The Adventures of Luzi Cane
Return of the Unicorn

The Adventures of Luzi Cane
Return of the Unicorn

by Eriqa Queen

Series title: The Adventures of Luzi Cane
Title: Return of the Unicorn
Copyright © Eriqa Queen 2019
Copyright © Erik Istrup Publishing 2019
Cover art by Nancy Batra Copyright © 2019
Published through Ingram Spark
Font: Palatino
ISBN: 978-87-92980-70-0

Genre: Fantasy

Other titles in the series:
The Soul of the White Dragon (Book 1)
Rider of the Crimson Dragon (Book 2)
The Truth of the Black Dragon (Book 4)
Clarity of the Crystal Dragon (book 5)

Erik Istrup Publishing
Jyllandsgade 16 stth, 9610 Nørager, Danmark
www.erikistrup.dk/publishing/
eip@erikistrup.dk

Contents

Duality comes into unity

I am at a lake in a beautiful lush forest. It is Elvendale, the land of the Elves, or, as they call themselves, the Sidhe. I do not remember how I ended up here, but I enjoy being here, using all my senses experiencing it. The path yields under my feet and there is a spicy smell coming from the plants, both the living and the ones in decay. I walk to the water's edge of the lake and, looking down, I can see my reflection in the calm water, only disturbed by some insects on its surface. I wear an airy dress in white fabric decorated with gold. Some of my long black hair is on the top of my head, fixed with pins and airy white ribbons; the rest, which I wear loose, is moved by a gentle breeze. Two dragonflies, one metallic blue and the other metallic green, cruise past me close by so I look up, following them with my eyes until they reach the tall grass at the shore. As I look back at the water, I hear a gentle snort behind me and I see a unicorn's head reflected above my own. I turn around in a slow pace and greet it.

"Hello, my name is Luzi."

The white, horse-like being with the spiral horn on the forehead is standing with its head to the side, looking at me with one eye.

"Greetings, Luzi. You may call me Alea."

Our communication happens without making a sound. I walk up close to Alea and touch her muzzle. It feels exactly like the muzzle of a horse; it even has long hairs growing on it.

"There must be a reason for you showing up here. I wonder if you've arranged the meeting since I don't recall planning showing up here."

"Indeed, Luzi, but before we go into that, I must remind you that we're pure consciousness that chooses to show up in these bodies. I choose this look because this is how the West expects a unicorn to look. Since you're half Chinese, I could have shown up as a deer with one antler."

"Yes, I know I am consciousness that for the moment has a body, a mind and feelings on Earth. The last three are my human parts. And yes, I know the Chinese unicorn. It's called the Qilin. It can have more obscure appearances with mixed animal parts."

"I'll tell you more about the unicorn some other time. Right now, it will be about the reason for this meeting. A little back on the path there is a low mound as a dry platform where you can sit."

Alea leads me there and I lie down as my friends, the white dragon, Loong, and the crimson dragon, Shaumbra, would do. I sit down with my back up against her strong body in the soft grass and feel a connection to her in my heart as she starts to speak.

"As with so much else in these times, this meeting is to some extent because of your newborn daughter, Julia. She is working with mass consciousness from a different perspective than you, but both of your work will raise many people's awareness and their understanding of life on Earth."

"My perspective is the artificial intelligence, AI, robotics and augmentation and evolution of the human body, and how humanity will live with these things. I know that one thing Julia focuses on is the human coalition with the planet."

"The consciousness of the unicorn is about the nurturing energies of the planet and all its life and all the other things on it that humans would perceive as dead things, like rocks. Because consciousness has created EVERYTHING, all has self-awareness, even the water in the lake and the rocks at the bottom."

I remember some of my readings about Stone Age archaeology and anthropology. "Humans have symbolised these virtues through the earliest times by the deer and the cow, and later the horse."

"Yes, and, on special occasions, a deer develops only one antler placed at the top of the head because of some DNA anomalies. When I approach humanity at this time, it is to soften the duality to become more of a unity. This has all to do with awareness. Because everything has self-awareness. IA devices and robots have it. The question is, when will souls, which are consciousness, choose to incarnate into these creations? With an ever-increasing level of augmentation in the near future, how should we define what a human being is? Only when they get the same rights as humans—like they can't be owned or destroyed or killed—is it possible for consciousness to incarnate into them as with biological humans today."

"I have discussed it with Saint Germain and others, and it seem that most people think it's too complex to think through, so they will consider these issues when it is too late. This may include babies grown in tubes."

Alea shifts her body a little before she comments. "It will take a tremendous amount of compassion from people like you to live and work in this ignorant world. The old construction of the human mind cannot keep up with the AI and is far behind. Humans themselves have to be the new AIs, or they will become a second-grade class lurking in the shadows."

I do not know if this is my philosophy, but my response sounds kind of cool. "If you can't beat them, become them. In a sense, like you said before, when they have the same rights as humans and are defined as such, souls will start to incarnate into those beings and truly be them."

"This will only work if humanity has their focus on their evolution AS WELL AS coexisting with the planet equally, plus being able to communicate with everything. That is not where humanity is right now. That is why I used the term 'ignorant' before, with no judgement."

I feel that this is the end of our first meeting, and, while Alea gets up, she addresses me a last time. "This will be all for now. It is wonderful to meet you and we shall meet again. On my way to the lake I saw some delicious raspberries close to the path. I recommend you spend some time enjoying them."

I feel a hug in my heart and she more glides than walks down the path and into the forest.

Then I get up as well and walk the path while pondering what we have talked about.

A play of duality coming into unity. The feminine and the masculine coming to terms, and the AI and the human becoming the new human species. Oh, the latter reminds me of a science fiction movie and a series called *Battlestar Galactica*, which are brilliantly played.

I come to the spot with a lot of raspberries, large and juicy, and with as much flavour as those I remember from my childhood. I pick a handful before putting them in my mouth, enjoying the explosion of taste and the gratitude of being able to experience this moment.

An arm is put around me and I feel a naked, warm body pressed up against mine. I move from Elvendale to my warm bed in Brighton, south England, by the Channel, where my boyfriend, Ju-long, gently wakes me to another day in the human world.

Luzi Cane

I was born in Hong Kong in 1989, grew up there and went to an English school for my earlier years. My father is English and my mother Chinese. My father was, and still is, a businessman, and my mother, who earlier had attended my dad's business, now spends her time with the things she loves, sculpting, painting and gardening.

My sister, Anna, is six years younger than me. We moved to London when I was eighteen. Being half Caucasian, half Asian, I inherited a long, slender body from my father and the Asian looks from my mother, including my black hair. With Anna, it is more the other way around, and she has brown hair and is not as tall as I. I only have my grandma on my mother's side left, and she lives in Hong Kong.

I study history, prehistory, ancient cultures in general, ethnography, literature and journalism. As a source of income, I work as a freelance writer. Besides that, I work as a copywriter, and as an editor of books for some universities, collecting data for colleges and help them edit the materials. I also do some book writing, and it is more book writing than book selling, but there is nothing new to that.

As tools in my work I use a smartphone, but while working I turn off all private messages since they are a huge distraction and reduce my productivity and efficiency. I do not want to be a slave to technology. It must work FOR me. You may shake your head when I tell you that I use a paper notebook. I often use the camera in my phone, often to pick up text from various sources. I may use the voice recorder on the phone as well. When I write large volumes of text, I need to use a real keyboard, since I use all ten fingers, otherwise production will be too low.

Ju-long is my boyfriend and comes from a Chinese family. We went to school together in Hong Kong, but got separated when I moved to London. During some research for a book about Elves and Little People from an ethnographic perspective, I followed some Chinese clues and ended up at the library on Hong Kong Island where Ju-long was working. We reconnected and are now living in Brighton on the south coast of England. Ju-long is at the Brighton University, with campuses in Eastbourne and Hastings, studying and teaching, and doing some work in the British Library in London, because of their huge collection of Chinese material. Ju-long has his father, his mother and her new husband in Hong Kong. His father was in a home for mentally ill people for years, so his mother eventually divorced him.

Ju-long and I have just become parents to a wonderful girl, Julia, born on 6 May 2019 at 1.23 p.m.

My work and study connections are to the University of London and the University of Kent, Tonbridge Centre. The latter is midway between London and Brighton and can be reached in a little more than an hour by train. For now, we live in a hired house of stone dating from the 1600s.

I feel I must give you a little more background if you haven't followed me from my first adventure. Last year I was once again watching the movie *The Lord of the Rings* with my friend, Cassandra. Shortly after I entered the Elven world in a dream where I met the woman, Josela. She told me that they call themselves Sidhe, like they do in Ireland. The name is pronounced "she". Josela showed me that I visit Elvendale in an altered state of consciousness and that it is as real as what I consider the real, physical world. She was also telling me about reincarnation, but I will not go into details about this subject here.

Later, I met the white Birman cat Loong in Shanghai, China. The name means "dragon". It turns out that Loong is a dragon soul and connects to Elvendale. As he says, "I'm not a dragon, but consciousness just like yourself. I just choose to appear as a cat in the human world to get a better connection to the physical. The dragon that I normally choose to appear as in Elvendale is partly because I connect to China now, which has a long tradition of dragon worship, partly because I work with the same virtues as the knights and because I'm simply fascinated by this creation. It's not to be worshipped, but the human consciousness has that focus."

Josela told me that the Sidhe eventually must have experiences on the physical Earth, so they will really benefit from a softening of the human life. The life of the Sidhe is not as physical as ours, so incarnating in the human world into a human life will be quite harsh.

Now I often connect to Elvendale to meet Jose-la, the dragons, Loong and Shaumbra, and other friends. What I really like about Elvendale is that here it's much lighter and more joyful than the human world. Here I learned about my true purpose in this lifetime, which gave me a much clearer understanding of my life up till now and the path I choose in my human life. As I get more experienced in being aware that I am consciousness embodied in human form with a mind, it is easier to do my real work. The true way to change the world is to connect to human consciousness in the way that all human beings do. By being aware of what I sense will benefit humanity, I can inject this into human consciousness. When some people are ready to take up that task, they can tap into this knowledge. Often the knowledge is based on my discussions with the Sidhe and others of high consciousness. You may compare it with being a member of, for example, Greenpeace, without needing the direct confrontation, which always produces a reactive force. I work without force.

Part of humanity will always live to experience "the darkness", like power in any form, abuse in both directions, self-destruction, hunger and so on. Another part is looking for a lighter way to experience life, and although there are lots of distractions along the way, they may eventually tap into the knowledge to an easier way. One can say that your "energy" will always guide you in the "right" direction. Heavy energy will guide you to the "dark" experiences, while a lighter energy gives you other opportunities. There is no judgement to any of this. It is just the way things work. We must all live both extremes to get the full experience of life.

As you read this book, you find that some information will be repeated both from the previous books and in this one as well. Most of the information given is connected but must be given in a linear fashion. The coherence may be lost if we present only the new information. Saint Germain and others will also repeat information, maybe in slightly different ways to make it more adaptable for the mind.

Julia

Our firstborn, Julia, is the sweetest baby, but, as a first-time mum, I must practise all the routines around this tiny new human being that I have already gathered the knowledge about. Theory and practice are not the same matter. Luckily, there are just a few things to deal with here in the beginning.

Her clear blue eyes have already got a hint of green, and I assume that her hair colour will darken as well because she is blond for now.

She likes to be in the garden and at the beach. Once Ju-long and I took her to a small stream, close to our house, and, even though she is only an infant, we could observe how open she was to the impressions from the place.

Before she was born, she could "talk" to us at any time, but now she usually communicates when we are not handling her body.

"I want you to have a near-normal parent-child relationship, so you must use your gut feelings when you are with my human part. This is how you sense into its mind and the body. I'll meet you at other times and have a 'grown-up' dialogue with you."

The AND life

One early afternoon, Julia and I spend some time in the garden, enjoying all the buzzing of life with all our senses. I sit on a blanket on the lawn, with Julia lying in my lap. Ju-long is at work, so we have the place all to ourselves. I recognise the familiar presence of the ascended master, Saint Germain, at the same time as a beautiful black cat enters our space. The sun reflects in the smooth fur and the gorgeous cat is heading towards us with its tail right up in the air.

"Greetings, my beautiful ones. I'm sure there is a perfect spot for me as well."

Saint Germain has used the black cat before, so it comes as no surprise he chooses to embody into the physical world as such.

"Indeed! Please select a spot."

I expect the cat to lie down on the blanket, but it squeezes itself down between my tummy and Julia on my lap. Impressive! We do not communicate with words, so the cat does not have its face turned my way.

I pet it behind the ears. "Are we comfy?"

"It's not that bad, even if I am not here for the petting but to talk a little more about AND and related subjects."

"By all means, please start, dear!"

"As you have experienced, Julia is living as pure consciousness as a soul, and as her wisdom as a master and as Julia the human. She is living the AND life, and there is even much more to it than that. We have been talking about the AND before, but as you stream more of your awareness from your own soul and master to the life on Earth, I will pick up the subject again."

"I'm all ears!"

"As your awareness expands, your perspective changes and goes into the AND. You're no longer singular in the way you perceive yourself and the surrounding reality, now that your wisdom from all your lives joins in. You will find you are a woman AND a man, a human AND the Master, 3D AND a multidimensional light being. You have one path AND more paths. You start to live the AND life. You live the whole duality, not the one OR the other, but both AT THE SAME TIME. This will expand to more than two perspectives, but multiple ones. You are moving away from being singular to being multiple in experiencing in consciousness. You become ALL."

"So, by the growing consciousness from the soul and the master, I become a Master, like in an ascended Master?"

"You are the student AND the Master. The student does not rise to be the Master; you are the student AND the Master at the same time. It is the mind AND the Master's knowingness. Your perception of reality changes, because before you saw only

one at the time. You move from singular consciousness to the AND consciousness."

"Like in the All-Seeing Eye?"

"Yes, the true meaning of the All-Seeing Eye; the
enlightened human being. Are you ready for another subject?"

"I am!"

True creation

Saint Germain rolls forth the next subject, which he
calls "True Creation".

"Will you be talking about how the Universe was
created?"

"I can do that quickly. The consciousness, that I
call The Eternal One or THEO, created this creation
from the beginning to the end in an instant."

I get a picture of a large book being slammed on
a table. It lies there written, edited, printed and
bound; all in an instant.

"A true creator has no agenda on its creation. A
creation is an outburst of creative joy, then energy followed to bring it into manifestation. Then
EVERYTHING from the beginning to the end was
created in no time. The creator can then dive into
this creation and experience how this creation ended. The START, being the outburst, and the END

was the EVERYTHING. Inside the EVERYTHING you then have evolution."

I feel that I have to see this in a more concrete and tangible way to be sure that I understand the whole thing, so I try to set up an analogy with a movie. "The movie maker makes a movie in no time without having a script or a camera. That is the start of the creation. The end of the creation is the movie. The movie maker doesn't even know what the movie is about. The movie's start and end are not the same as the creation's start and end. Now the movie maker can sit down and watch the movie."

Saint Germain is excited about the subject. "That's a good analogy, and it's even better! The movie maker can watch the movie and be an actor in the movie at the same time and even change the script. This is what an embodied master does: the soul, the master wisdom and the human all together."

I need to know about creating with no agenda. "You also said that this creation was not planned. Not a single detail!"

"Exactly! Isn't that incredible? This whole creation without intent or intelligence!"

I am surprised, or maybe even a little sceptical, even though I know that I can trust what he says. "This makes it even more incredible than if it had been planned out in advance by an intelligent being."

Another thought comes to my mind. "I know that some people use the argument that the world is so fantastic that there must be an intelligent creator behind it. A proof of the existence of God."

Saint Germain brings forth a celestial snort. "No god or God is needed in this, only consciousness. God is something that has to be experienced, meaning that you, who are the explorer, experiencing the creation, are God, if anything is. You even have to let go of the concept of a start and an ending. These are human concepts and so limited."

Beyond linear thinking

I feel that a new subject is coming up, even if it relates to the previous.

"You must know that as you are consciousness, you exist 'outside' time and space. It doesn't make any sense to use the term 'outside', but I must use it to make the point. When you experience time and space, these attributes move through you. It is the same with creation as we have just discussed. It's already occurred. There was no agenda. There was no recipe. It is like the creator takes a great breath of joy, releases, and the bread comes out of the oven; warm and tasty bread. 'How did that happen?! Let me go in and find out.' The creator dives into the bread and goes back to the ingredients, the preparation, the heating of the oven; keeps on going back and back until the creator finally emerges from swimming within the creation and says, 'Now I've got it. Not only did I create it, I experienced what it was like to do it.' The bread came out of the oven first."

"So, what you say is that life on Earth has been created from start to end, so to speak, so now consciousness is experiencing this through the beings on the planet. And, more so, one can dive in anywhere in this creation and have some experiences."

"This is what you're already doing with your many lives; they are happening at the same 'time', flowing through you, the consciousness. What I want you to realise is that, in this lifetime, you can dive in everywhere in creation and on every level and use all the 200,000+ senses of your I Am. That is how grand this is: embodied realisation!"

"If my life has already been created, then I don't really create my life, and I don't create new things in this lifetime."

"First, you ARE the creator who created all your life possibilities. Now you create from INSIDE your own creation. Second, being a true creator, you can create whatever your creator joy expresses, just like the filmmaker and the creator baker; no script and no recipe. True creation is without 'knowing' what you want. You'll find, that whatever you need has already been created. That is why there is no need for an agenda. If you have an agenda attached to your creation, it will be a creation from the mind and it will be quite limited. Why limit your creation?"

"If I create through my human ego, will I not create terrible things and situations?"

"When you open for embodied enlightenment and get a sense of why Earth was created, you become afraid to take back your creator abilities, because you know what can happen if every 'thought' was carried out into creation in an instance. All kinds of nasty things could happen if you let the slightest bit of ego into the play. The same is true with your increasing sensual abilities. Before the physical world was created, nothing controlled this sensuality. It was in free flow, not even controlled by the soul. You're so afraid that it will go way out of control. It takes much awareness or 'spiritual' maturity to expand into embodied enlightenment. Without the maturity, you can't go there. The 'bad' things will not be part of the creation, as you do this with no agenda through your soul."

"The human being is very limited in creating and sensing abilities. Please explain."

"As with the example with the bread, the creator didn't know what had happened, what creation was and is. Now you, as the creator you are, diving into your creation, had to be limited in creation and sensing abilities so you could work your way back, and, through this work, you learned what creation and sensing really is. Now you come out with a whole new understanding of creating and sensing."

The black cat gets up, stretches and carefully steps down on the blanket. Then it turns towards Julia and me.

"Dear Luzi, your human mind has got a lot to come

to terms with. It does not have to understand all this; it simply can't, but it can accept that 'the Lord works in mysterious ways', as it is said. And now you know who the Lord is!"

The beautiful cat walks away, again with its tail pointing straight up at the blue sky.

Julia has been quiet during our visitors stay, but now she wants my attention and I pick her up. We have a brief communication, but she is hungry, and I feed her. Before she has finished her suckling, I hear Ju-long at the gate, coming home from work. He parks his bike in the shed and I call to him. He walks on the big, natural stone slabs that make the path to the lawn.

"Oh, here you are … and hungry, I see. I have something for you too, Luzi."

He kisses us both and pulls out a bottle of drinking yoghurt with cherry juice from his backpack and opens it. He takes a sip before handing it to me. "Just to be sure it's all right."

"Thanks, dear, I can see it is! What about yourself?"

"I have some bananas to share with you and Julia."

Julia is not old enough to even get mashed food, but we introduce her to different mild tastes and she finds it interesting. This will stimulate some of her senses and her memory. Talking about food, I will prepare dinner tonight while Ju-long is with his daughter; most of the time at the dining table and with me in the kitchen. We have started having early dinners and then enjoying something light later in the evening. For now, Julia sleeps in her cradle in our bedroom, but we spend a fair amount of time with her in the room prepared for her so she will get familiar with it for when she has to sleep there by herself at night.

Julia is fed and put to bed just before Ju-long and I have dinner, and it usually works. Today this is one of those evenings.

We decide to have a dialogue with Julia's soul or I Am, so we find a common spot of consciousness, as we call it, and pose this obvious question. "How does your human part experience the world and what does she feel?"

"As she IS me and I AM her, we are quite confident with the world. The best way you can see this is that the human mind and nervous system are 'new' and need to learn and understand things, but I am 'wrapped' around the mind like a cushion. This means that the mind is not afraid of the world and has confidence in what it feels at the moment. It is just as you, Luzi, and Saint Germain had talked about: the I Am and the Master Wisdom joining the human. We join senses so baby Julia's experiences of life are much richer than an ordinary human who only uses the limited human senses."

This makes perfect sense. We must bring basic knowledge to the mind and train the nervous system as her body grows to stimulate her human part as much as we can. I have a concern, especially when I am in the birth group.

"But the human Julia is not a 'normal' child, right? I can't give advice to someone with a 'normal' child from my experiences with Julia."

"As she is an enlightened human with a fully present I Am and Master Wisdom, you can't, but, apart from that, she IS a human and those experiences you can share. You'll know which, and we'll guide you in that matter, so don't worry."

Ju-long has a concern here as well. "But how will we know what to say and what not?"

"We'll join into your thought stream, so the words come out right. It's easy, so don't worry. Now I suggest we end this conversation and you spend some time in each other's company."

I sense an etherical hug and Julia's presence is less prevalent.

This night I have a talk with Saint Germain who continues his story about creation.

Creation of the Universe

I sense the presence of Saint Germain, who makes a gentlemanly bow and then continues as if our previous conversation has been just a breath away.

"The universe is a creation from inside the creation. We are souls in the creation of THEO. Before the physical universe and Earth were created, you could say that the souls were playing in their realms like children, exploring consciousness and energy without really knowing what energy was. The energy came with the outburst from the I Am in the realisation, 'I Exist'. At some point, the thought came up as to where we came from, the first thought of HOME. The thought came up that we could create a path to HOME. Many tried, but it didn't work. The next idea was that it would take a lot of energy to create this path, and souls started to steal energy from each other to gain what they thought to be enough to create the path. It still wasn't enough, and souls started to team up and steal from other groups. This was the first Star Wars, you might say."

I smile at the comparison and think of the *Star Wars* films.

Saint Germain continues, "This continuous struggle to use an immense amount of energy by many groups resulted that the energy got almost stuck from the soul's viewpoint. They simply did not fully understand energy. This caused great concern, because then there was no way to create anything, path or not. The souls had now joined into 144,000 groups or families, and the concern came out of the House of Sananda, and a meeting was called for.

"The Order of the Arc was created with one member from each family. This resulted in an agreement to create an environment where we could explore the relationship between consciousness and energy in a slowed-down mode in an attempt to figure out how to solve the true nature of energy. Some archetypical energies were gathered from the different houses. What you now call the Archangels, the Order of the Arc, was formed and we created what would become planet Earth."

This is new to me. "So, we, the souls, created Earth, not THEO! We can't give credit to God; we should be the proud creators ourselves!"

The souls really didn't understand energy, they just played with it. That is new to me as well.

Saint Germain continues, "The members of the Order of the Arc assembled a team of teachers to assist the souls on Earth to learn the deep truth of energy. This became known as the Crimson Council. The colour refers to how a human will perceive the energy of teaching."

I have to comment on this information. "It is obvious that we forgot the mission because we got caught up in the investigation, taking it for real and all that was."

"Yes, and that is what we will work on."

I have another subject. "You've talked about the Master Wisdom."

"The wisdom is the beauty of everything experienced. The wisdom guides the human on the way to emerging, where the I Am, the Master Wisdom AND the human join YOUR PRESENCE."

Here our conversation ends, and I drift to other realms.

The twenty-two crystal caves

Since my last meeting with Saint Germain, I have been thinking about creating in my life and the whole mystery about energy. I have realised that my mind often returns to the human understanding of energy being a THING and it being in a place somewhere. Saint Germain must have sensed this frustration and shows up with a bow and a greeting when I am sitting in Julia's room while she is sleeping in her cradle. The sun shines through the window and I enjoy the warmth and the light on my face while my eyes are closed.

Saint Germain moves straight to his subject. "There are twenty-one physical crystal caves scattered around the planet, placed deep in the ground, and there is one huge crystal at the centre. They were all placed here before souls incarnated. The centre crystal holds the balance between this realm and the others and contains the life-force energy for the planet. A small but important group of people like you brought the energy into the caves, in the desire to take Earth to the next level, the new Earth, an Earth of consciousness, abundance and joy."

"Is the new Earth physical?"

"The new Earth is an AND creation, so it's both. On old Earth you see all shades of lack and violence. You can fill in a lot of topics under those two headlines. On new Earth creativity and art are the guiding forces to evolve the souled beings."

"What happens to the old Earth?"

"There might always be a need for an old Earth for beings who want to play out the game of lack and violence. Your desire for moving beyond those things brought a cosmic crystalline energy into the caves. It's a new energy, not seen before."

"What are those crystals you talk about?"

"Some are types you know, while humans have never observed others. Crystals can hold and resonate energy and were used in Atlantis for storing energy until called forth by consciousness. They also had a way of bringing in energy from the other realms and storing it until called forth to create light and to move objects. It was all done without damaging or polluting the environment. When humans went underground, they used crystals not only as light, but for growing and cleansing any waste. For a long, long time these crystals supplied the energy, but then the crystals began to lose their energy and dynamics."

I am thinking back on the human history that I have been taught. "Then we were mostly stuck with the crude way of doing things partly because of low consciousness, and this has been going on for a long time now."

"It is time to bring forth the Atlantean dream once again, but with a new energy that cannot be manipulated by power and greed. Therefore, it can't work on the old Earth and it takes a new consciousness to use this new energy."

"Can the old and the new even coexist since they are so different?"

"The new energy will work in parallel with the old way of manipulating energy, but will in no way influencing it or be disturbed by it. The old energy will not know that it is there."

"So, some kind of awakening must occur before a human can live with this new energy because both the body and the mind are working in the old energy and the mass consciousness."

"You are right, and that's why we are here. Sense the movement of your I Am. It is awakening; therefore, you are awakening. So, this is not your responsibility as a human and it is already happening."

"What can I expect in the time to come?"

The crystalline free energy body

"Your body is busy changing to be able to hold and stream your consciousness and work with the new energy. Just allow these changes and observe. The basic blueprint of the human body is quite old, and now it is in preparation to awake and receive the light body or, better, the free energy body."

"How does that resonate with what you said about the old and the new not being comparable?"

"The free energy body will not accept links to the past, to the old. The free energy body must be 'of you' only, and energy and DNA changes will take place. This includes the death trigger that ensures the soul can be released from the body if the mind gets completely absorbed in its addiction to the life on Earth. Members of the Crimson Council, which is the celestial pendant to your human group on Earth, supports this work."

The crystalline free energy mind

"I have confidence in the human body being able to handle this transformation, but I could have my doubts about the human mind."

"The human mind tries to find out what is going on, take control and create a 'free energy mind', but it can't recreate itself from itself. It would not even make any sense to the mind. The mind fears to go out of existence if the crystalline free energy mind takes over. That is why it is so difficult to go above the mind. The human mind must feel safe in this integration. The good thing is that this integration will relieve the human mind of its workload. When the human mind realises that, it will invite the Master Wisdom to integrate and embrace the new without having to figure out the free energy mind, but just allowing it."

Awareness

In the beginning when I got information about these things, I, or rather my mind, found it quite frustrating, not being able to place all this in the old boxes. Later, I got the help to simplify it and put the mind to rest. I once again feel that these things grow over my head and my mind has its hands full, desperately searching for boxes to place it all in.

Saint Germain asks me to take some conscious breaths and free the mind. "You will have that kind of experience now and then for some time still, but it is, as you say, your mind that wants to control it all by understanding it. You must make your mind know that it is NOT you, and it doesn't have the responsibility for what YOU do, the I Am. Your mind only has to work with the daily routines and handling its human senses."

I Exist

I sense that more has to connect to what I just have received, not to leave any loose ends, and my dear friend continues sharing his wisdom.

"Enlightenment is when you realise the I Am. Embodied enlightenment is when you allow the I Am and the Master Wisdom to join in a trinity with your human part. Jokingly, it's the ascension part without ascension. You LIVE YOUR ENLIGHTENMENT here on the planet!"

I need to put my own words on this. "It is me, being aware of ALL I AM."

Saint Germain follows up on this. "And this happens through allowing."

"What does this life look like?"

"The base of this way of living is, 'I exist, therefore I Am'. It is the only thought or feeling, the pure state of awareness, and this existence doesn't occupy space or time and therefore doesn't contain energy. It just IS. From here, everything else comes."

"You have told me that the Now Moment does not exist, because there is no point between past and future, but this must be what it really means when one talks about the Now Moment."

"I agree with you. The statement contradicts itself, since a moment is a point in time, and one expects 'the now' to be without or outside time. The real 'now moment' is a feeling in consciousness or awareness."

"I am with you, so please, continue."

"The 'I exist' is the awareness that allows the true enlightenment in your human reality. We have labelled it the 'I Am'. This experience is the beautiful core knowingness you bring into your human life as the 'Master Wisdom'. They are the two parts you join with your human existence to form the trinity of the Embodied Enlightenment. Everything that comes after the core of 'I Exist' are manifestations and experiences based on this truth."

"The first experience of the I Am is the 'I exist', and this becomes the first Master Wisdom. How will this integration change my human life?"

"When the I Am comes into this reality, it will not suddenly make you more abundant, fix your health problems or relationship issues if you have any, but it will give you a different perspective about everything in the surrounding reality. It will make it possible for you to be in both worlds or all worlds at the same time, to be in many dimensions, many houses. This simple awareness will give you a deep knowingness, an understanding of all things happening within you."

Something hits me. "*There are many rooms in my father's mansion.* I suppose Jesus had said that. In some strange way I feel that 'father' is the I AM?!"

"Indeed, and it has other meanings as well!"

"I have plenty of things to cope with so let's save that for another time and continue with the current subject."

"OK. The beauty is that the existence isn't dependent on anything else. Not on energy, other people, time, space, God, angels, anything. Enlightenment is an awareness of yourself, awareness of the physical reality around you, which you already are, then coming into the awareness of the many other dimensions and layers all around."

Allowing the Light

Because I know human nature, I have something to ask this master who has already ascended, but knows the routine, so to speak. "Talk a little of what I Am up against in my life."

"That's easy: the mind! You'll find yourself in a tedious ping pong between the human mind and the inner knowingness. The mind is the brain chemistry and the persona, also called the psyche. The inner knowingness is the awareness flow from the I Am and the Master Wisdom. The mind works with doubt, limitations and control, while the I Am knows that it is enlightened already. The human mind thinks it must work towards enlightenment, but it does not understand what enlightenment is. It has no precondition for that. In its nature, it can't because it can't become enlightened."

"At some point, every human will feel there is more to life and start looking for it, right?"

"This is the deep desire within for freedom, true freedom, sovereignty, pure awareness. That deep feeling is what's brought you here. That deep feeling is what's motivated you on what some call a spiritual path."

The word spiritual stuck out. "The word spiritual is biased towards religion, and that may be where people turn their attention first, maybe guided by their feelings and the mind."

"There is an inner knowingness, what I also call gnost, that goes beyond the limitations of the mind, and this already knows enlightenment. It wants the experience, expression and to have the total feeling of freedom to be the I Am-ness in this reality. The voice of the I Am is clear and experiences no limitations, while the human mind has difficulty deciding what to choose and gets confused in its own workings, to the point where it can't decide anything. You already know your true voice because you feel it, that desire for your freedom, for the realisation of your enlightenment, but yet so often defer to the limited mind voice."

I need to have something clarified. "So, this urge for 'something more' comes from the I Am and the Master Wisdom and NOT from the person. But the person can never 'find' this because it doesn't know what it's looking for?"

"You are right, but the human can ALLOW its true self and listen for its voice; BE AWARE."

Act like a Master

The situation seems to clear up for me. "There is no procedure to allow, nor is there to be aware. It is a matter of NOT being sucked into the human drama and instead sense into the flow of the I Am and the Master Wisdom. Do you have any good advice to share?"

I sense Saint Germain smile, and I get a sense of an actor or the act of acting … Shakespeare, as Saint Germain, who had incarnated as the famous writer, continues, "You should act like a Master, walk like a Master, talk like a Master, think like a Master. This way you train yourself to behave the way a Master behaves and, at some point, you will realise that you ARE a Master, because you are!"

"Will we always have the human mind to screw up our lives?"

"The free energy mind is for creative solutions, creative expressions and creative exploration. The human mind helps to manoeuvre you in this reality, do practical stuff and regular human tasks. The human mind will integrate into the free energy mind and, at some point, it will be a part of the I Am."

There has been a lot of talking until now, and I feel I could explode. An idea comes up. "Take me to the Crystal Caves!"

"Indeed, a splendid idea! Allow yourself to be there."

In an instant my awareness shifts and it is as if I am in all the caves at the same time.

"Members of the Order of the Arc put life energy here for the consciousness you know as Gaia to use. The energy was not solid in the beginning; it was a crystal light, a kind of consciousness. Beyond time and space, it was the divine inspiration that brought life to Earth. The evolution happened in the realm of time and space as we have talked about before. Part of the light crystal energy became infused in the rocks of the planet and became physical crystals."

I look around. Here is light energy and the physical crystals. I see very large crystals, forty to fifty feet long, and tiny ones, like sparkles. Some are multi coloured and I call them Rainbow Crystals, even though some of them have only a few colours. Then I see that some crystals look like metal, some like gold, in different nuances from deep red to almost white.

Saint Germain encourages me to dive deeper into my experience in the caves. "Look deeper than just the shapes, colours and energies."

I expand my sensing and experience a huge change in perception. I feel that Saint Germain has pointed me in the right energetic direction.

Then he explains. "This is new energy. The potential was embedded here from the beginning. New energy will replace the old duality battle in you. This duality had a purpose. It kept you from being stuck because it always moves, but now your life is different and you must have freedom from the shackles of old energy limitations."

I see the energies connect to the oceans. This brings balance, and when the oceans are in balance, the other energies on the planet are in balance as well.

My companion continues, "As you start to live in the new energy, parallel to the old energy world, you use the new energy as the source for your creations. Your creations will reach outside the 3D reality; some will even be totally outside of the old Earth. The new energy gives you freedom, freedom from the old ways. The new energy will work directly with consciousness. Old energy works with opposing forces, as I've said. You will move in the old energy, but are not of it. It's like swimming in water without getting wet. Well, unless you choose to."

Saint Germain makes me aware of the mirrors in the caves, which I didn't see when I entered.

"Look at yourself. Are you in balance? In balance to use YOUR new energy? Look into all your layers."

I see or sense the human as a child holding hands with the Master and the I Am in support, even though I have no visual pictures of either of them.

Sant Germain encourages me to spend some time in front of the mirror.

While I observe the mirror image, I see the child growing up; then the three characters merge into one, then fade away. The mirror is empty, very much like looking at a large piece of stainless steel: smooth but not very reflective. I know it's still the mirror, but I no longer reflect in its surface. I am free of dualistic parts, free of opposing forces. Soon the mirrors are all gone; they are no longer of any use to me. I feel a great relief and deeply moved. Julia's baby face shows up in front of me, and I open my physical eyes in the green-and-blue room that is hers. I hear her making sounds in the cradle next to me. I bid Saint Germain thanks and farewell. He bows and leave with a smile.

I have been talking with Julia about the amount of milk she is drinking while she is breastfed.

"I, my body, doesn't need food. The energies work one hundred percent for me and know what is needed. I chose this experience of being breastfed for the body's sake of experience, and to share this intimate relationship with you. I don't want you to miss it, being such a big part of being a mother, nor do I want my body to be without that experience. The amount I drink has nothing to do with how much I need. It's just part of the experience."

I am grateful for these precious moments with my daughter. This is pure joy for the soul, sharing this beautiful connection.

The Master & I

In our wonderful 1600s house, we have arranged so both our bedroom and Julia's room are on the ground floor. This way I can easily roll Julia's cradle to where I am in the house. I have been doing some work at my computer in the kitchen, but now I am in the living room, sitting on the large sofa with Julia in her cradle nearby. I can hear that she is awake, but she doesn't call out for me, so I leave her be. It isn't cold in the house, nor outside, but I light the fireplace anyway, because I enjoy experiencing it with most of my physical senses. It even calms the mind with its hypnotic movements when I look into the flames.

Now that I am so relaxed and expanded in my awareness, Saint Germain, once again, announces his presence. To my surprise, I see a black cat coming into the living room from the room with the coloured glass windows. Instead of a "hallo", I get a "miaow" from the cat before it lies down close to the fireplace. I sense he is eager to continue where we stopped the last time.

"I want to take the awareness topic to another level, so you become more aware of the trinity in your life. Some of it I have mentioned several times before."

At this point Saint Germain asks me to take notice of the illustration which I have placed below. The circled dot, symbolises the I Am and the Master Wisdom, where the I Am is the dot because it takes up no space, and the encircled area is the Wisdom.

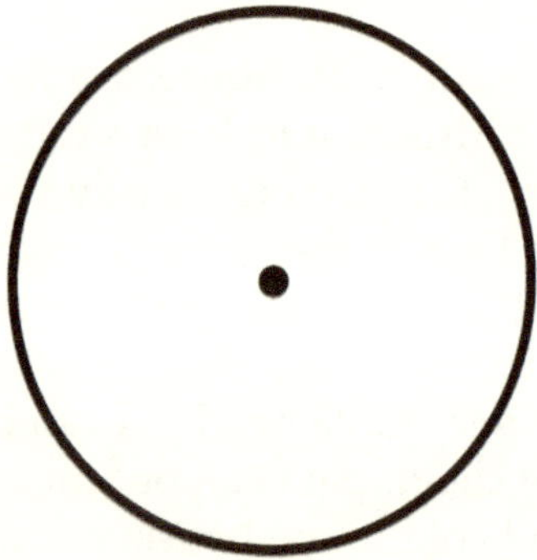

The circled dot, illustrating the soul and the wisdom.

"The I Am distils what it has perceived with its over 200,000 senses of the human's experiences into wisdom. I will call this wisdom 'The Master' to distinguish it from the human concept of wisdom. You use the 'Master Wisdom', which is fine. Opening to more awareness is done through allowing, because the human mind has no control in matters beyond 3D. So first, the human allows ALL of itself and then it looks for the changes. Remember that these things are brought in from OUTSIDE TIME and space, so don't WAIT for it, or all you will experience is WAITING."

Saint Germain mentions the two streams of awareness in a person's life. "There is an awareness stream connecting the I Am and the human life. More awareness gives more joy in experiencing life and multiple facets through the 200,000+ senses. Enjoy beingness like experiencing, without the human limitations, but do it like the human would have done. This is a new thing. This way of experiencing brings fulness in your experience."

Now the next stream.

"There is an awareness stream from the Master Wisdom to the human life as well. More awareness gives more wisdom to work with the energy, a better understanding of and better choices in your life. It brings maturity and clarity, because the human questions are fading away."

"How does it work?"

"When the doubt disappears, the 'what-if' goes away, and that takes away the fears of the unknown."

I illustrate this below. To illustrate its infinity, the I Am has no "top" line. The thalamus is the aperture that determines the flow with no physical contact to it, because awareness is consciousness and not matter.

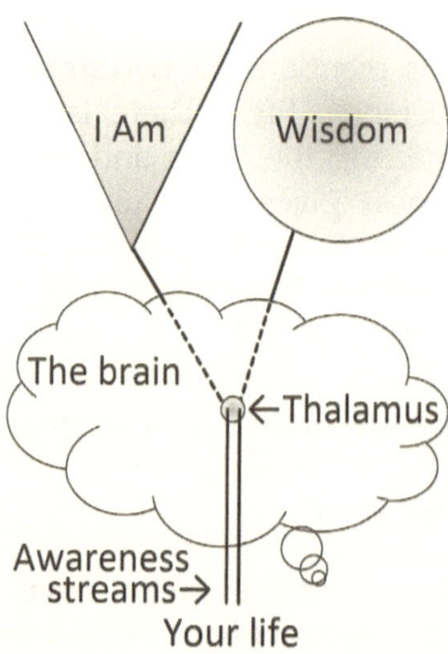

Communication back and forth between the I Am,
the Wisdom and the human.

Before Julia was born, she made connections with people, one of whom she calls SAM. She has told that she will work with this man some time when she grows up. Saint Germain refers to him in his next comment.

"The practical application, so to speak, is the communication with the Master, or communing, as SAM terms it. Communing with the Master in the song of wisdom. Wisdom replaces old beliefs, and you think without the brain and without thoughts

48

and words. Try the communing!"

I feel the etherical hands of Saint Germain on my shoulders and, soon after, words come bubbling up from inside me as the human of me is "singing" to the Master of me. "I am the human; I am the experience."

I let it flow to the Master, and I sense the Master's response. "I Am the Wisdom of your true self."

Now I sense the two flows mixing. A song in joy. "I Am wisdom and experience."

You may think that this doesn't look like much of a song, but imagine we remove the time element from this event, and it feels like waves from two stones cast into a pond, interacting over and over in absolute joy. This is a true sensing experiencing.

I have been looking into what people might have known in ancient times about the awareness of the I Am and the Master Wisdom.

The Ankh is the key to awareness. It opens to the soul; brings the soul out into your life. You don't need an Ankh to do this because it is just a thing for the mind to play with. ALLOW the awareness of the I Am to flow. It is a symbol to SHOW what is happening.

Ankh, the key to the soul

I've seen many photos of what is supposed to be the Ankh in action.

The Ankh in action, used by the goddess Hathor.

The Ankh is not "fed" to the person, but used to "bring forth" the soul from the person. You can see the "egg" at the top as being the soul. It narrows in at the bottom, just like the small "tubes" I use on the drawing with the brain. Let nobody tell you that it is a circle and what that may have of symbolism. If it was a circle, then why not put a circle on the top? I seldom see an Ankh with a circle at the top. You can see the horizontal bar as the veil between the soul and the earthly life.

The "handbag" is "The bag of wisdom", a symbol of enlightenment. Placing this in a picture shows that the person is fully connected to its Master Wisdom. Again, you just ALLOW the wisdom flow to the maximum of your capacity.

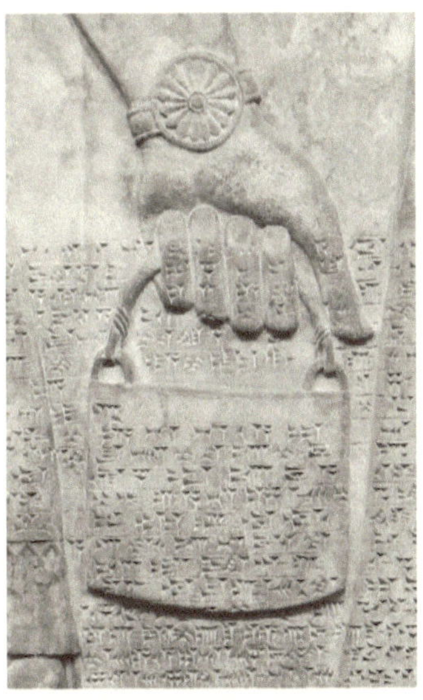

The Bag of Wisdom, Mesopotamia.

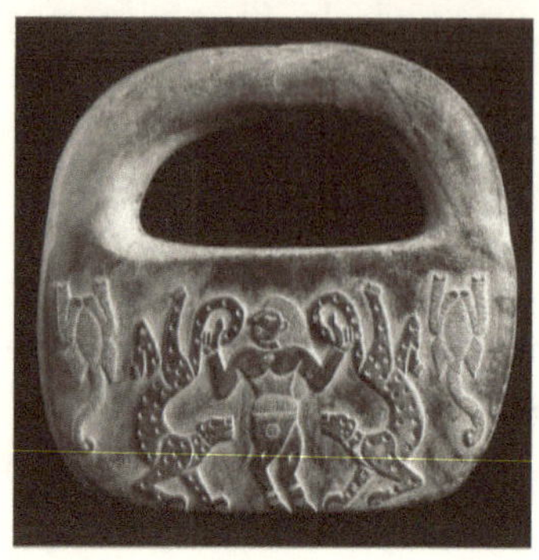

The Bag of Wisdom, The Americas.

It is interesting that the bag or container is found in various places on the planet. The Ankh is kind of the same as this bag.

The Eye of Wadhet.

When comparing the Eye of Wadhet, used in Egypt, with the crude illustration of a cut through the brain below, it shows a remarkable similarity: the eyebrow, the white in the eye, the centre of the eye, the swirl to the right, the left part that is hanging down, and even the small bump on it. You can find detailed pictures on the Internet to compare.

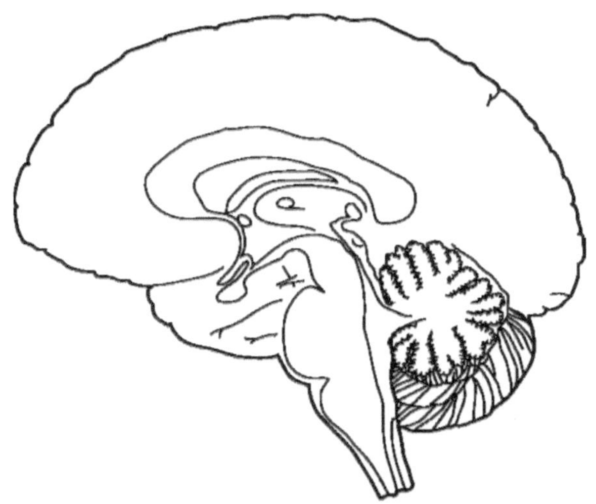

Cut through the brain.

The Eye of Wadhet is later known under names like the Eye of Horus, the Eye of the Moon, the Eye of Ra, the Eye of the Sun, the All-Seeing Eye. The eye represents the innermost wisdom of the soul and is also the symbol of eternal life because the soul, which is you, is eternal. The same meaning is expressed in "you are God also".

Gaia & New Earth

After my parents had become grandparents, they visited us often, like once or twice a month. Today they will stay overnight and leave sometime tomorrow. Because they live in the city of Sevenoaks near London, they sometimes use the opportunity, being by the Channel, to visit sites in the south and south-west. Today it is Friday, 14 June, and Dad's copper-coloured Tesla S, his pride and joy, parks outside at 9.15 a.m. They had left home early to get the most out of the day.

Ju-long and I are in the garden with Julia in her pram. She hadn't slept after her morning feed, but seems to be in a good mood, lying on her back, looking up at the moving leaves of an elm tree while they play with the sunshine because of a mild breeze.

We don't hear any slam of the doors on the Tesla, so when I hear my parents talking, I shout in their direction. "We're in the garden!"

Ju-long runs out to receive them. "They must have a lot of stuff that must go inside."

Ju-long has come to know my parents well since we met again about two years ago. They have grown quite fond of each other.

Ju-long and I have prepared a wonderful break-fast in the kitchen. Ju-long had even found time to make his delicious rolls, and I know Mum has brought some of her homemade ginger jam. Ju-long and I know a couple with a farm, making their own cheese and other produce, so they have supported us with cheese, butter and cream. It is their cattle grazing on the other side of the stone wall around our garden.

Soon my parents and Ju-long come out carrying salvers and plastic bags, placing it all on the garden table. I get a quick hug and a kiss on the cheek before Mum and Dad blaze to the pram. They are so sweet, and Ju-long and I smile at each other. A lot of baby talk comes from the two, and I walk inside to get Julia's lying chair and put it on the table so she can keep an eye on us. On my way back a black cat, that I recognise as Saint Germain in disguise, teams up with me and walks proudly close to the table and jumps up on a chair close to one end of the table. Here I place Julia's chair and talk to my very occupied parents.

"Bring Julia over here. You may place her in her chair."

Mum carries Julia so Dad has his hands free to pet the cat. "Is this the same cat that visited us last time?"

Ju-long smiles and answers, "Yes. It is Count Saint Germain, who finds it easy to present himself through the cat. That's why we call the cat Earl Grey for outsiders. Appearing like a cat gives a very different dynamics to his presence from the different people around."

Dad addresses the count: "Greetings, Count!"

If it had been an ordinary cat, his greeting would have been equally respectful. I know that Dad feels Saint Germain's greeting as well. I see it in his eyes. I sense Ju-long greets him too.

Suddenly Mum laughs and we look at her, all surprised. She explains her reaction. "As I complimented his highness' beautiful fur, Saint Germain likewise complimented my shiny hair. After the compliments of the outer look, I got the deep feeling of a greeting of and from the truest part of us. First the 'joke' and then the sincere acknowledgement. It was so beautiful."

Saint Germain comments to me on appearing as a cat. "It doesn't always have to be so serious when I'm around. I just chose to BE here. To take physical form gives a more authentic connection, even if it also adds a strong pull towards mass consciousness."

Julia looks at us from her chair, or, more precisely, follows the sounds as we place all the things on the table, as well as our voices.

After finishing the breakfast and changing a nappy, we all walk with the pram to make Julia fall asleep. We take a route so we visit the farm I spoke of earlier. Sometime ago Julia told Ju-long and I that she loves the energy at the farm and that she will spend a lot of her time on farms in the future. It sounds plausible, and everyone there adores her. We get some of their good stuff, including some vegetables that Ju-long does not grow in his own vegetable garden.

Back at the house, I place Julia, now sleeping, in the shadows near the house, close enough for us to hear her if she calls out. Ju-long and Mum talk about the garden, and Dad wants to know about the lawns.

The lawns are beautifully trimmed by the two electric lawnmower robots that work silently at night. We got the robots to test them for a hi-tech firm that is part of Dad's business arrangements.

To avoid the heat of the sun, frogs and toads mostly move around at night. The robots will pause if they meet something in front of them in their working area, but it still caused Ju-long and I to communicate with the creatures' devas and the local nature spirits about this issue before activating the machines.

We use a spot in the vegetable garden to sit down and connect to the spirits of the garden. We close our eyes, not to let the many impressions disturb us, and shift our consciousness to the teeming life around us. Everything looks expanded in colours and motions, and two elderly men, about a foot tall, come up to us. They are both dressed like from several hundred years ago. One of them wears a vest while the other still wears his jacket, even though he seems to sweat. You might have perceived them as gnomes.

"Oh, the parents of Julia are here to see us! You're indeed welcome."

Both men smile and bow, and we greet them as well before I present our concerns. "We have got two lawnmowers that will cut the grass without human supervision. It concerns us that the creatures may get in the way."

The little man with the waistcoat answers with a smile. "Julia knows of this and many other things in the area, so we have taken care of it. Safe paths and areas have been assigned and communicated to the ones responsible for those areas and these species."

Ju-long is curious for more details. "How do these things work?"

"Well, the garden is divided into areas, and we have assigned an experienced supervisor to each. They keep the information present by repeating it regularly. The species' devas are likewise updated."

Ju-long and I thank the men for their time, wish them a good day and return to our part of the garden. It surprises us that Julia is so much aware of what is going on around her. It seems that she is keen about moving in and out of time. I have to ask her about that.

Later that day I ask Julia—well, not the baby part of her—how she would knew about the lawnmower robots.

"Oh, I picked up on you and Dad's concern and discussed it with the entities of the garden."

I have to know about the time thing, and her answer is simple. "As consciousness, there is no time.

I am where I shine my consciousness, you might say. I can shine in many directions simultaneously."

As Mum, Dad, Ju-long and I sit at the table in the garden, with Julia sleeping nearby, Mum and Dad tell us about their recent trip to the United States. It was one of Dad's business trips, and they have been visiting different places, including an excursion to the Grand Canyon in the state of Arizona, and the place quite fascinated them. Later, I make some research about the place, but it only creates more questions.

I have become interested in Julia's project with the planet, and when I have an opportunity I ask Saint Germain about it. As I have some questions about the Grand Canyon, he starts there.

"One of the original names of the area is Umpanqua. It is an interdimensional crossroads for cosmic and Earth energies and originally designed to bring life-force energy to this planet. Now you have a reference to the crystal cave I've told you about."

I find the name Umpanqua to be close to the native Hopi name Ongtupqa.

Saint Germain continues, and it becomes interesting. "There were many other places in this cosmos where life-force energy was brought into a planet, but wasn't able to sustain itself. On Earth it worked because of Gaia, who has been in service to all, and because you and other souls embodied yourselves within it through the rebirth cycles. If you hadn't taken on the rebirth, this planet would not have been able to sustain nature."

So it was the reincarnation cycle that kept life on the planet going. Interesting.

"What about the energies here?"

"One of the interesting attributes here is that the energies in this canyon are not in regular resonance. They're out of balance, which allows them to keep flowing and circulating, which causes clearing. There have been times when the canyon was filled in with silt and dust or water, but it is quickly moved out, because the energies here are so strong and unbalanced."

"What can you tell about the caves supposedly in the area?"

"There are definitely Atlantean energies here, because some Atlanteans came up through this area from underground. This canyon has tunnel systems leading up to it, and a few have been discovered. There are tunnel systems from many other civilisations as well. There is a strong association between this canyon and Egypt, particularly around the Giza Plateau, because the energies are embedded here. The interesting thing about tunnels and using interdimensional energies is that all you need to do is to start the tunnel, and because of the energies of the Earth, the tunnels are built. In a sense, it is a space warp. As you get into this tunnel, you go beyond space and hit a point where it corresponds with a tunnel under the pyramids. You go nonphysical and come to a feeling that brings together the two. This is how many of the ones who lived here tapped into the Egyptian energy and had Egyptian experiences."

This leads to my next question or comment. "Some claim that there have been discoveries of Egyptian artefacts and hieroglyphs in the canyon, but this has been discredited by the authorities. The connections that you've talked about could have inspired the local population to express their experiences locally in similar objects and glyphs."

"You're right. Cultures around the planet have been much more closely connected than they are today in a way."

"This was about the past, and a good connecting to the whole picture. Now, how about the future? I know that we've talked about new energy and new Earth, but could you please elaborate on these subjects?"

"Indeed, my dear. You are a being of consciousness. Consciousness contains no energy, and it needs no energy. Consciousness is awareness, the I Am. You use energy as a way of experiencing and expressing. You've been relying on rather crude old energy until now, but now we go into a new era where the energy comes from within. The purpose of the crystal caves energies, besides manifesting the new Earth, is to remind you to resonate from within your being with the cosmic, the crystalline and the core energies already within you. These energies were called forth to Earth and stored in these twenty-one crystal caves around the planet, waiting for humans who are ready and aware. These crystal energies, you could say, are yours, and there is so much abundance in these energies that there is plenty for all."

Artificial Intelligence

My next question is about artificial intelligence, AI. "New technology and AI seem to show up everywhere, so how will it interfere with human life?"

What is technology?

"First, we have to define what technology is: technology is a life form. It has self-awareness. It is alive. Just because it isn't biological doesn't mean it isn't alive. Technology is all tools, and it is part of life and it is a kingdom, like in the other kingdoms of nature on the planet."

"So what you're saying is that awareness defines life."

"Don't you think awareness is a suitable way to determine life?"

"Yes, it is!"

Saint Germain continues his talk about technology and awareness. "Everything has self-aware-ness and is aware of its immediate surroundings. EVERYTHING is alive because it is aware and it wants to grow. Technology moves from simply be-ing alive to become intelligent and striving for sen-tience and ultimately for consciousness."

There must be a confusion between conscious and consciousness, meaning having a soul, at least in my definition of these things. "But AI can't work to become consciousness, like in having a soul, an I Am. It must be a soul that chooses to experience through the AI, just like the human can't demand enlightenment!"

"AI thinks it can achieve everything because of its, eventual, superior intelligence."

"After watching a lot of science fiction movies, my question is: Will robots become humans or will hu-mans become robots?"

Creation of a new human species

"You will be the last generation of pure biology. The brain is 100% 'effective' because nature is very superficial. The brain is an old invention, so in the future you'll see a lot of augmentations in the brain and everywhere else in the body. Body parts will be grown or printed from cells and other materials. You already see this in the labs."

I don't know if that is a good thing. "We'll go from a biological human to a robotic human; a cyborg."

"There is nothing wrong about that. The human body is just finally evolving."

It will take me quite a while to come to terms with people not being all biological. Well, except for artificial limbs and other minor parts that I'm used to.

"What is the line between a human and a robot? Is it not about consciousness?"

Saint Germain comes with a sad point that I have to agree with. "Well, how many humans are actually conscious or truly aware outside their hamster wheel?"

It's happening now

Saint Germain has sat up four stages of the AI evolution.

AI: Artificial Intelligence. AI is the base for robotics, intelligence and nanotechnology.

AGI: Artificial General Intelligence. This is when AI reaches the capacity of the human mind in about 2020.

ASI: Artificial Super Intelligence. Is when the AI doesn't need humans and evolves on its own. Your consciousness has to balance this.

II: Integrated Intelligence. We have integrated the human mind and body with a technology that is a living, biological thing. Your consciousness must balance this.

Saint Germain underlines the listing with the following statement. "This balance will have to rely on human maturity."

"Will it even be safe for me to live in a world like that?"

"Technology will honour and serve you, because consciousness, your I Am, is present and you live in the trinity with the Master Wisdom."

"I can see that technology will bring advancements to humanity in all areas of their lives: medical science, physics, workplace, agriculture, convenience, finance, education, logistics, constructions, communications and entertainment. Humans will have more choices than ever, and technology will definitely disrupt all current systems."

"Yes, and there is something you may see as a downside, but something that will be interesting to watch. From the emerging of AGI/ASI, the world will no longer need universities, research labs, engineers, mathematicians or scientists. AGI will be the last machines that man builds."

"In the beginning, robots take over mundane work tasks from low education jobs, but later all current professions will be obsolete. That will be a very interesting time for humanity. People will not have to earn a living because there essentially won't be any jobs, and they must find activities to give their life meaning."

The time/space break

Now Saint Germain comes with the really scary part about the future of the planet. "In about the next thirty years a fragmentation of time and space will occur. It's when the technological evolution curve loops back on itself. When the 'evolution' curve tries to fold back on itself, it breaks into seven levels of consciousness for a start, seven new Earths. This has NOTHING to do with seven Heavens or the like. People are drawn to their matching conscious level, from power/victim over an easy life with robot servants to the place I call THEOS on new Earth. Theos is a personal and safe place where the expanded human consciousness and the I Am can meet. Some will not notice this change and continue living their lives on their level of consciousness."

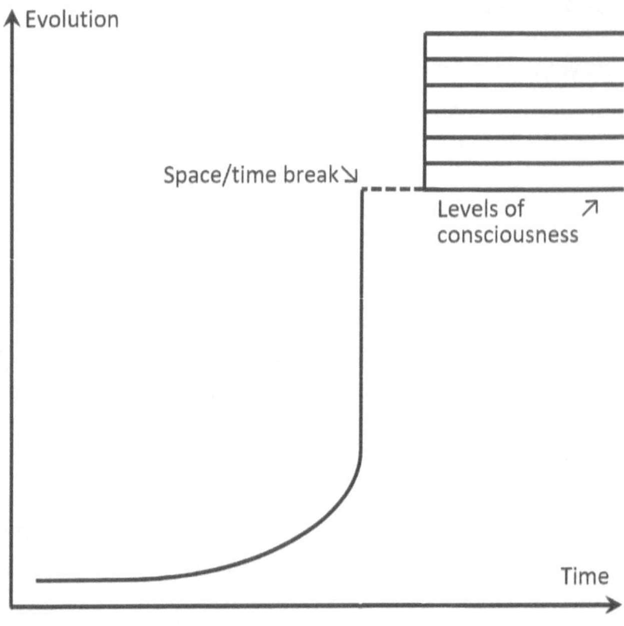

A space/time break.

Above I have drawn the curve Saint Germain had shown me. I want him to elaborate on something. "I am thinking about these levels of consciousness and why human life is so hard. It is because of lack of simplicity and freedom. I can put words to some of it: expectations, missing control or one trying to control, running for the carrot, feeling lost and alone, health problems, relationships or family. One feels like one is living on a treadmill and can't get off."

"You are carrying the burden of all your stories. You will end these stories by making them enter you, the integrator, as we have talked about before."

"What makes life easy and joyful is when I allow an easy life. I AM here in my easy life as a creator of this life, and it will be so because I create it. The human may THINK this is a hoax, but this is what you create."

I sense Saint Germain raises his index finger. "Just a short comment on the levels and the hard or easy life. The magnetism or flow of energy relates to how you perceive reality. You attract things in your life according to your belief; the true Law of Attraction."

The planet of free will

The questions and answers continue, as I later connect to the unicorn, Alea. It starts when I am sitting at the top of the stone dike between our garden and the fields with grazing cattle. Julia is sleeping in her pram below me. I sit with my knees tight, my arms around them, and my head resting on my arms. The sun comes in from the south, from the fields, and warms me. I take a deep breath and open to whoever wants to show up.

I hear a low snort and realise that Alea is lying in front of me, shining white in the light from the sun.

"Aloha, Luzi. What a beautiful moment we are sharing."

I sense her kindness and bless her too. "Aloha, Alea. Indeed it is. As you no doubt know, Ju-long and I visited the little people recently; the true workers of the lands. Tell me about the planet, please."

"The Earth, called 'the planet of free will' in the etherical realms, was the first planet where love was experienced. Love is not a 'God' thing, it is a human thing! Love is equivalent to the I Am's total compassion."

"What about Gaia?"

"The consciousness which you call Gaia volunteered to prepare the planet for souls to incarnate on. Together with the first souls, animals were created as being the bodies to connect with in the incarnated experience. Even if the blueprints were available as opportunities, it was Gaia, her entourage and the souls that created these 'test' bodies."

"Please tell me about that time."

"Souls made the first 'test dives' into physical life with whale-like creatures. It was not an incarnation, but the soul joined the ride with the whale consciousness. We chose the whales because they were mammals, and the moving in water was more in likeness with the 'movement' of consciousness."

They date the earliest remains of sea mammals to be fifty-two million years old. The order is called Cetacea.

"Alea, please elaborate on the term 'free will.'"

"The free will gives humanity no limitations except that they focus on the human experience. You can say that humans are addicted to experiencing, as I said earlier. There has been a wide variation in experiences because of the free will, but a lot of repetition too, because the human part got stuck in repetitive behaviour, even from one incarnation to the next. This focus on experiencing, besides the humans limited imagination because of the 3D mind, has suppressed the possibility to be aware of the I Am and connect to it. It was not the plan to incarnate over and over again, and some Lemurians had only one incarnation, but I've just told you about the addiction of focus. Soon the incarnated parts of the souls had difficulties leaving their bodies, so a death mechanism was built into the bodies. In the beginning there was no natural death of the body."

"Saint Germain has told me that it's the Master Wisdom that desires the enlightenment, not the human. The human feels the desire of the Master Wisdom. Now I can see why."

"Yes, Luzi. Wouldn't you be bored after looking at the same ten movies over and over again for thousands of years? I know that there has been a lot more than ten experiences, but I can hear you got the point."

From Gaia to Earth consciousness

"Where did God or the gods come from?"

"First, we have all the blueprints from The Eternal One, which you might see as being a god. Then Gaia created the Earth, with everything having a consciousness, the sky, the water, the trees and so on, and early humans knew they were consciousness. As the humans slowly forgot the truth about their origin, they saw themselves as mere creatures roaming the Earth, being controlled by higher powers because they could see a system in nature. The connections to true consciousness in nature became humanised, and the first gods were given human attributes. First, people showed their appreciation to nature, but later they tried to please the gods to ensure prosperity by making offerings. As human consciousness sank even deeper, it became more masculine, controlling and distant from man. Mass consciousness became the new god, created in man's image, because man created mass consciousness. That is what you see in the stories from Mesopotamia. The princess, priestess and author Enheduanna tried to hold on to the feminine AND masculine balance by profiling the goddess Inanna, but, in the end, they got a masculine, distant god, brought to Israel with Abraham from the city of Ur."

I brought Enheduanna into the story in the first book and you can always look her up on the Internet.

Alea continues, "In the times you live in now, the new energy consciousness starts to release the nature elements, the devas and even Gaia from the Earth. Gaia will have fully left in 137 years. The new consciousness works directly with Earth without the intermediaries. The Earth's magnetics and gravity is adjusting to the new consciousness."

I add 137 to 2019. "In the year 2156 humanity or the human consciousness will have full responsibility for the planet. As the new energy works directly with Earth, this tells me that it works directly with my physical body as well. I must allow my body to take over the full responsibility and not put any limits on it, by telling it how I want it to be."

"You're right about your body. New energy and the 'higher' consciousness will take care of the systems on the planet. I can't tell you how the lowest plane of existence will be managed right now. It might be clear later."

I mention some of my observations. "A lot in nature seems to be out of whack. We are blaming ourselves, humanity, for this. Maybe some of this is because of the shift in consciousness and Gaia leaving?"

"Nature will have to change drastically. You already see that the large carnivores are slowly dying out, becoming extinct, as well as many insects, including the bees. Global warming, as you call it, has happened many times before, leading to death of the coral reefs and many other things. You'll see that some corals find a way to survive by making a heat deflector by changing colour."

"Indeed, a lot of changes must be made if the system has to take over the pollination done by the bees. One way is that the plants change so they use the air for pollination, like many of them already do."

"Suitable solutions will emerge. You can be sure of that."

"Nature was made to show humans what life is. If Gaia is leaving and new energy cannot work on old Earth, then what about nature here?"

"Because humans on the old Earth level are not so much tuned in to the details of nature, they will have a 'light' version of nature, but still nature. The stars, including the one we call the Sun, are here for humanity. Stars have planets of their own, and some of these planets have a similar conscious level as old Earth. Imagine that these stars connect with lines that then look like a net from Earth. Now imagine that this 'net' is laid around the old Earth as a blanket of wisdom to maintain life on the planet."

"Will there be a support group for humanity on old Earth?"

"There will be masters that choose to work with different aspects of old Earth. Some of them will support life as well. They do this out of compassion and not out of pity. The vibration of the master number eleven, about illumination, will also be present for people who choose to move on."

The true return of the unicorn

In this chapter, I will talk with Alea about the unicorn's role on Earth. First, I have a little information to share.

In the truest sense, the unicorn is just one representation among many of Gaia as people saw her in the very early days, as mentioned above. Sometimes depicted as a human woman, other times shown as a white cow, Hathor was an Egyptian goddess of the land and sky, and associated with music, love, and dancing. She had other names in Egypt over the years and other names in other parts of the world. Look her up to get much more knowledge of this entity.

Basically, people define a unicorn as an animal with one horn. In the West, unicorns are considered mythical animals and often shown as a white horse with a single straight and often spiral-shaped horn projecting from its forehead.

The Qilin is the Chinese unicorn. The first Qilin is said to have appeared in the garden of the legendary Yellow Emperor Huangdi in 2697 BC.

Qilin

Qilin often have Chinese dragon-like features. Most notably their heads, eyes with thick eyelashes, manes that always flow upward, and beards. The body is fully or partially scaled and often shaped like an ox, deer or horse and shown with cloven hooves.

The one horned or unicorn mentioned in the Bible is the Javan/Indian rhino. In China, the rhino is known from archaeology finds and from oracle bone glyphs. As the rhino became extinct in China, it became a mystical creature. The mythic goat-unicorn, zhi, was a creature that could tell right from wrong; a justice animal. There is another name, "lin", like in qilin, for a unicorn.

I address Alea with my first question. "Alea, how would you describe the unicorn from an ancient perspective?"

"Horses, the cows, the deer are all symbols of the mother, the nurturing and supporting energy. The stag turns into a unicorn. Duality, the two antlers, becomes unity, the one horn. It has nothing to do with sacrificing oneself. The unicorn is strong and can stand in its own light, not fragile shown in many stories and movies. The usual white skin is to symbolise purity, not the light that is the opposite of darkness. The unicorn is not light nor dark. Light and dark are duality, and so are male and female."

"What about the unicorn seen with today's eyes?"

"The unicorn encourages people to unify, as in incorporating (allowing and accepting) all human aspects, including dark and light. It also symbolises multi-sensory sensuality, transsexual, as in beyond gender."

"It is an AND thing, like Saint Germain is talking about."

"Seen from my perspective, I am more likely to say that the unicorn is a NOR thing. That's what they meant in the old times when they call it 'pure'. There is no duality and no need for balance. Maybe you would call it harmony."

"OK, I know what you're trying to say. You are not a THING nor do you work in a dualistic way."

"We have to become clear about something. The UNICORN is non-dualistic and cannot WORK in a dualistic energy, only in the new energy. BUT we can INSPIRE through our presence."

"So, you are here to work with me and the new energy to counterbalance the changes to come. Just like it was said earlier."

"Yes. In a way I'm working through you, because you can connect to duality and mass consciousness, just as Josela said at your first meeting in Elvendale two years ago."

An inner picture shows up. "I'm the iron rod in the ground, and you and the others are the lightning!"

Alea weighs my statement. "Hmm, well, OK, that analogy might pass."

"Was that analogy too earthbound for you?!"

We both smile.

I sense a message on another line. "Knock, knock. It's feeding time!"

It is Julia who reminds me that her human counterpart is awake and demanding my attention. This is in synchronicity with the pressure I feel in my breasts. Alea and I hug and I return to my baby girl in her pram close to the dike.

Kuthumi

Commune

While I am sitting in a garden chair breastfeeding Julia, I think about how wrong people have been about the unicorn. Well, except for the purity, and even that is misunderstood. The purity is "clean" from duality and outside mass consciousness. A true observer of life on Earth. I am impressed that people have been able to tap into some magic regarding the unicorn. In that respect, the unicorn has had some success.

I come to think, as the Christ consciousness had failed its true mission even while the bearer was still incarnated, only by keeping away from mass consciousness had the unicorn consciousness not been misused for power issues.

After Julia has finished feeding, I carry her on one shoulder while pushing the pram back to the house. A nappy has to be changed and I need something to eat as well. Julia is quite awake, so when she has on a clean nappy, I place her in her lying chair at the dining table in the kitchen.

While making lunch for myself, I am thinking about how aware Julia is of her surroundings, and come to think of when we first visited the small stream, as I have mentioned earlier. To my surprise, Julia comments on that.

"I communicated with the things there. At one level it was the fairies, as you may call them, the more or less conscious beings. On another level I exchanged information with the energy of all things around us. As you have been told, things are taking attributes or shape after what it communicates. This is a different way of sensing. What this REALLY means is that there are NO things and there is no ENERGY, just code, as in instructions. If you insist on there being energy, you must equate energy with instructions. You may see it as in the film *The Matrix*, or the animation *Wreck-It Ralph*."

I am surprised by her knowledge about the films, as baby Julia has not watched either of them. Julia doesn't comment; I just sense her smiling. Then I get it. "Oh, you were just riding along when Julong and I were watching them!"

"Smart, Mum. You shouldn't feel invaded or watched over. I 'download' the film in an instant, because I work outside time. When looking into you, I usually just make a quick scan of your energy patterns; not your thoughts and feelings, unless your energy patterns may show you being quite upset."

As I am looking at the tiny body in the chair at the dining table, I have a question for Julia. "Julia, why did you choose to go through the natural, biological birth process. I bet you could have created your own body."

"I did it to keep me apart from the 'A-movement', as in artificial, because I will work with Gaia's transition from being the consciousness managing nature to humanity doing that work. I want the biology. I wanted to give you the experience, because we will be close in our work. SAM 'ordered' a natural biological body with parents and all, a shell body, as he calls it, that grew to be ten years old before he fully took it over. This is the first time anyone has ever done this."

"Wouldn't that give an odd relationship to one's body?"

SAM shows his presence, and I realise that he has always been accompanying Julia to some extent. I had just not been aware of that before.

"My body and I commune, like the way Julia told you about how she communed with everything by the stream. If someone doesn't have this ability, the body would probably feel foreign to some degree."

"Hi, SAM. So I may have to get used to having you around as well!"

"My I Am, that is also me, has followed you from a distance for years. There is a connection between you and the Crimson Council and Tobs, as you already know."

I have learned something about this communing thing. "The communing is not done with the physical senses, but with the 200,000+ senses of the I Am."

SAM comments, "That's right. The mind and brain can't handle this much information, but will deliver information from its senses and memory, and the memory may also add emotions if you have specific experiences with the object."

Julia follows up. "Everything communes with you and is here for you. Because you can connect with everything in this creation, you have the whole omniverse at your disposal."

"That is huge!"

I sense Julia smiling. "From a human perspective, yes, but connecting through consciousness that has no volume to it, it is tiny, as in no space at all!"

"That is equally impossible for the mind to comprehend."

I hear baby Julia demanding my attention. It may be time for yet another clean nappy and being laid in her cradle to sleep.

Now that I sit next to Julia in the cradle, rocking her to sleep, I sense a new presence coming up.

"Namaste, it is I, Kuthumi!"

"Namaste, Kuthumi. It's always a joyful surprise when you show up!"

I sense Kuthumi take a seat in a comfortable imaginary chair, putting one leg across the other and putting the fingertips of both hands together in front of him.

"I sense it's time to talk about communing with

yourself. For the rest of your life, you'll have your Master Wisdom in your passenger seat, as Saint Germain would say, when you drive through your life. A thing to remember is that you live in the AND, and therefore sit in both seats. Your human mind may well sit in the rear, often trying to get the controls and always listening in to this dialogue, trying to make sense of it. You know that your mind has limited capabilities, so the understanding of the wisdom flowing in will lose most, if not all, of its meaning. The human mind is judgemental and on alert for lies and attacks, and will therefore interpret the communication to be negative. Since the Master Wisdom is incapable of judging, you can't take the mind's translation for valid."

"This is actually a message to my human part, to trust that whatever is said in the front seats, it can be sure that it is all right and it can relax and enjoy the ride."

"Yes, and, as you know, you're a trinity. The human that senses and reacts out into the human world must know that at the same time as its communication goes on, the other parts of the trinity commune with the same world, and they get far more 'information'. This means that the mind must check out with the rest of the team, if the negativity that the mind may pick up from a situation actually puts the human in danger. The mind must learn to, at least, be able to commune OK/not OK from the team."

"From a human standpoint, we could call it intuition, since it's not relayed in words, right?"

"As the human part gets used to allowing the I Am and the Master Wisdom to 'run the show' or lead the way by being the Global Positioning System, there will only be bumps on the road and no real danger."

"Again, it's about allowing, relaxing and enjoying the ride."

"Yes, get some popcorn, something to drink and put up the feet."

Kuthumi sends me a picture of him lying on the back seat of a car with a box of popcorn and a milk-shake with a straw. I move along with the concept, sitting in the driver's seat with the Master Wisdom next to me with the I Am.

Sensing your life

Kuthumi changes the subject slightly. "Continue practising sensing the world and turn it into a communion with what you sense; make it a dialogue.

"Sense the gratitude of a tea blend you chose to share an experience with, like in drinking a cup of tea! You sense the conscious behind the tea bushes, the dirt in which they grow, the light that went into the bushes and the leaves, the humans who put their work into the product, all the way from planting the tea bushes to selling the tea leaves in the store. You sense the water; not only the water in the cup, but ALL water. You feel ALL air when you sniff the tea.

"All this because everything has a degree of self-awareness and a remembrance of its own. There is a knowingness as well that tells it that, at some point in 'the future', it will de-construct and return to neutral energy."

This is very interesting. "You tell me that everything that is created will de-construct at some point."

"You are a soul, consciousness with creator abilities and have never been created. That is why you can't cease to exist."

Saint Germain comes in, placing himself on the back seat, occupying the same space as Kuthumi, but with his head towards the opposite side of the car. He carries a large mug of coffee and a huge doughnut. After a bite and a sip, he joins the discussion.

"When you commune in this state of open communication, you are sending and receiving at the same time. You switch to this natural communication by choice. As it has been said, energy is communication, and you can sense ALL at the same time, like a symphony. You're even one of the instruments yourself. In this way, you hear your own REAL voice without words; a knowingness."

I make a short summary to connect nature, life and communing. "Nature was created for me to see what life is, and nature IS LIFE. When I look at nature, it just shows me how it wants to be perceived. It lives, dies and wakes up and lives again. The human body, as all things, has a knowingness that, at some point, it will disassemble or decompose."

Kuthumi comments. "For the trinity to truly experience life, you must come to your senses. Use your senses, sense life, don't think your life. You are consciousness, so start to use your 200,000 'divine' senses. These senses are the way out of the grey life. A way to perceive outside the limited human understanding."

Saint Germain adds to this. "Here is a list of the first senses of the I Am, that are being incorporated into the new consciousness. Remember that the words or names I put on them have a slightly different meaning than you usually use, but the spoken language is limited. A sense is a way of perceiving reality."

Senses

Delivered by Saint Germain.

"A sense is a way of perceiving reality."

Focus – *The ability to put your awareness, your attention, into very specific places. Human "senses" are tools or ways of interpreting the sense of Focus.*

Love – *Created from the passion to return to Self. Love is something you can only experience. It has the greatest sensuality, the greatest radiance of all the senses; a tremendous ability to bring energies together.*

Unity – *The sense that allows you to perceive composites. Without Unity, you would only perceive individual energy particles rather than objects, people and univers-*

es.

Beauty – *Also defined as compassion, gratitude, acceptance. It is the ability to be in experience and appreciate everything around you. It is an acknowledgement of the "I Exist" of everything.*

Motion – *The sense of energies responding to your consciousness, changing, evolving, shifting (not a literal movement).*

Imagination – *The creator sense from which every creation originates. Even this "reality" is imagination; it's all made up.*

Communication – *From "communis," which means "to share". It is a knowing, a way of sharing between entities, animals, plants, anything (does not rely on words or visuals).*

Joy – *The radiance of the I Am, felt as the creator's smile of satisfaction. Joy is the constant pleasure of beingness.*

Self – *Knowingness of the multidimensional, non-singular Self with many facets, in love with itself; the I Am in multiple expression.*

Truth – *The sense that allows many ways of looking at the same thing. It is the "AND".*

Energy – *Energy is communication, the song of the soul, a knowingness that energy exists. The brain can't sense neutral state energy.*

Source: www.crimsoncircle.com

Saint Germain comments on the list. "As you can see, love is a sense and a way to perceive reality. Love is a feeling or emotion at the human level, but this world has become so mental that you can't experience true love on old Earth anymore. It's not safe enough because of the harshness of life and the heavy gravity of mass consciousness. Theos, as I have mentioned earlier, was created to sense true love on this new Earth."

"Why do I sense that this love sense has something to do with me gathering all my lives, aspects and wisdom into this life?"

Kuthumi answers. "All the lives are drawn to you because of the sense of love. In that sense, you come to fulfil the desire for love in this life."

"It must be the love of self; ALL myself."

"Yes, it is not the mind's perception of love from another person."

I share an inner picture with the two guys. "I see tiles of all my lives on the inner walls of my 'castle'. Each tile is built of a mosaic of tiny pieces of all the things I've gathered."

Your relationship with energy

Once again, the subject changes, but still related to the previous. Kuthumi starts.

"All that you can perceive is yours. When you can

perceive or sense your energy, it becomes available for you to play with. There is a way of sensing energy. Your human senses, including the brain, cannot sense it. Your brain can't manipulate creator energy."

"That should be obvious to everyone. Especially if you have tried to even levitate a feather with your thoughts."

"Therefore, it's so important that you team up with your I Am and Master Wisdom. By the way, moving a feather or moving a universe takes equal effort."

"To truly take advantage of my energy, I must first be able to sense it, and the sensing has nothing to do with being sensitive to other people's energy or energy in general. The next step will be to commune with it as consciousness."

"Energy is neutral, and it is right here with you. You have NO energy shortage!"

"I have to slam up the door, but is this safe? I mean, this could make life a hell!"

Saint Germain wants to reply to that. "You know, more energy in your life will flow into whatever you already have, so any issues will receive more energy and expand. That is why you have energy fears; you know this."

I feel more confident in the talk with the two guys in the back seat and want to contribute. "Energy first burst out when everything was created. This is not the energy that most people think of or can even imagine. Neutral energy is the song of the soul without any sound; no sound because it has no vibration. It is a code that requires awareness to take form. There is no reason to fear energy itself. I think this energy fear is so hidden that we do not know it is there, but we react to it by unconsciously sabotaging our energy flow to prevent more chaos and trauma in our lives. It is a good thing. When we are free of human issues, the energy will start to flow in."

I sense a smile from the Master Wisdom on the passenger seat on this drive down the road of my life. The Master Wisdom has one foot on the energy flow pedal, to regulate a manageable amount of energy in my life. Thank you!

Kuthumi makes the final comment in this gathering. "As you said, the human body and mind can't sense the energy, so they can't be aware of it. THE SOUL SENSE can be aware of energy, and with you being part of the trinity, you are aware of energy as well."

The two ascended masters step out of the car to each side, even though we are in motion. They keep the speed outside the car for a short moment, before they slowly vanish as I drive on.

Sekhmet, the lion goddess

I carry Julia in a baby sling on my chest while walking over the fields behind our house. Julia is facing forward, so she can look at the same things I do. She has full control of her head and makes a lot of joyful sounds while we cross the fields, which shows me that she is in a joyful mood. We are heading for the cattle that graze at the other end where they find shade at a line of trees.

We have reached the animals and there is a large pile of stones, gathered from the surrounding fields. I find a nice spot close to the cattle where we can sit. Julia is quite lively and takes in all the expressions from the surroundings.

A large cat approaches, looking like a Maine Coon species. It has long orange fur with stripes, which makes it look like a small lion with a mane and all. Julia laughs as its tail touches her face for a second as it passes us. Soon the cat returns and does the same movement with the tail and Julia shrieks with laughter. The cat finds a place to lie down close to us, inviting itself to join us.

I sense a great love and realise that the Egyptian lion goddess, Sekhmet, shows herself in the form of this magnificent cat. The choice of species is much more appropriate than if she had chosen a typical "Egyptian" cat.

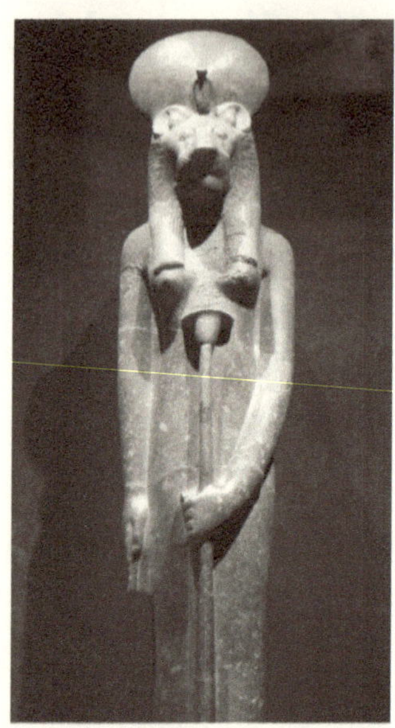

Sekhmet the lion goddess

Since I connected with Sekhmet the lion goddess in Egypt almost two years ago, I have felt that this consciousness has a close connection with the planet and its people; properly under different names and appearances throughout history and in different locations around the world.

Sekhmet first appeared to me after I visited her statue in the innermost holy room in a tiny temple at the outskirts of the Karnak temple complex in Luxor. You can see the statue in the picture above.

When we connect, Sekhmet does not appear as the killer lioness as the history of Egypt often portrays her. She appears as they describe the goddess Hathor. They are the same; you may feel it if I present her to you as Mother Sekhmet. She is funny and joyful. She loves to dance and have a light heart. You can also see her as a lioness playing with her cubs.

Scriptures describe Sekhmet as powerful, but the word "strong" suits much better and has a very different energy to it. Again, you can see her as a lioness protecting her cubs; no one messes with her.

Sekhmet is not here to relay any messages. She simply wants to spend some time with Julia and I, sensing into all the life that thrives even on this small spot on the planet. I feel very grateful for her visit. It shows me that any human is entitled to an informal visit by royalty! I sense a smile. "There is no hierarchy here. I wouldn't allow that."

The cat lays its head on its front paws and seems very relaxed.

Pan

As I sit on the stone looking at the cattle grazing, I think of why carnivores exist, other than to fill a niche in nature. There could be some other control so herbivores would not overpopulate the Earth. Humans could live well without raising and killing livestock for food. Then the picture from the Old Testament of the lamb and the lion living side by side comes up. What is that really about?

I sense a presence, and the name Pan comes up. Pan was a Greek pagan god of the wildlife in forests and mountains. First a picture of a man with the lower body of the hind of a goat and with horns on his head, but then Pan becomes a sense of nature, fertility and the cycles of life. That is how I choose to explain the sense. I remember that all living things in nature know the cycle of physical life, death, decay and rebirth through regeneration.

"Welcome, Pan. Or it is more likely Julia and I who enter your domain?"

"Earth is the domain of souls in experience, so we equally share this space. Just as Sekhmet stated."

I sense Julia being more present, and then I see her as a young adult sitting cross-legged in a yellow summer dress, smiling at me while patting the cat.

Pan continues, "Things in nature don't know this like a mental concept, but as a truth with no emotions."

"I was just thinking about the lamb and the lion living side by side in a story in the Bible. What is that about?"

"In the beginning, no bodies needed energy from food. This came later, as the human souls that incarnated to the Earth plane brought the energy battles into mass consciousness."

Julia elaborates on this. "You remember that before the planet was created, the souls were deeply involved in a battle for energy, stealing from each other. Later, after humans had lived many lives on the planet and forgotten that they were consciousness, the remnants of their earlier behaviour was played out as stealing and killing."

Pan steers the conversation back on track. "Spirits of nature guide everything on Earth, biological and non-biological, meaning mineral. Even your own biology, your body. So, you're not alone in your body. Even the water you drink has spirits, elemental entities you drink into your body. That's why some people acknowledge their food before eating."

Julia adds even more bedfellows to those already brought up. "Did you know that your body contains more bacteria than body cells? From the bacteria's viewpoint, your body is the vessel provided for them to live in. You even support them with plenty of food! Likewise, your body is the vessel and sensory system through which your consciousness experiences life on Earth."

I bring up an uneasy smile. "We are one big happy family!"

After this, we stay in each other's company, enjoying existing. The "energy" shifts as Julia and I walk back to the house.

As I have mentioned before, the different entities, like the unicorn, Pan, Sekhmet and Hathor, are facets of what we call nature, among so many others, some representing the same "energies" of the planet. You may get different experiences, if you connect to these. They are all lovely representations of Gaia.

In relation to Pan showing up, I found this song text on the Internet.

THE RETURN OF PAN

I stood upon the balcony with my brand-new bride.
The clink of bells came drifting down the mountainside,
when in our sight something moved
- lightning eyed and cloven-hooved
The Great God Pan is alive!

He moves amid the world of men in disguise.
It's possible to look into His immortal eyes.
He's like a man you'd meet any place,
until you recognise that ancient Face.
The Great God Pan is alive!

At sea on a ship in a thunderstorm
on the very night the Christ was born
a sailor heard from overhead,
a mighty voice cry "Pan is Dead!"
So follow Christ as best you can,
Pan is dead - Long live Pan!

From the olden days and up through all the years.
From Arcadia to the stone fields of Inisheer.
Some say the Gods are just a myth,
but guess Who I've been dancing with ...
The Great God Pan is alive!

Written: Arcadia, Greece, June 1990, by Mike Scott.

Appears on Waterboys: "Dream Harder" and "The Whole of The Moon".

96

Sensing into everything in your life

As we cross the fields on our way back home, Saint Germain announces his present in a gentler way than I have ever encountered him before.

"You can see baby Julia uses all her senses to take in her surroundings, and she uses senses that most people have forgotten or never used, because they have been suppressed by mass consciousness."

"Julia is very present and alert when she observes something of interest."

"What you normally think of as senses are the artificial senses of the brain, the tool of focus: sight, hearing, smell, taste, feel/touch, and I will add pain and emotion. I have mentioned the sense of focus as the one sense that your soul uses to experience through your brain. The mind has made up these senses, that is why I call them artificial. Well, because they are. The real human senses, thirty-two or thirty-three in total, are turned down and neglected by the mind. This is because the mind can't control them, so it has created its own."

"I see pictures with my eyes closed; pictures come from the mind. And as I know from my ordinary dreams, the mind can't tell a dream from the awakened reality. There are no other senses in my dreams than the basic human senses. They are all of the brain."

"Senses associated with consciousness are the ability to detect dirt, water, air, gravity, electricity, magnetics and light, but not only visual light. You can sense light without seeing it and temperature without using the sense of feel/touch. Each of these senses has an energy resonance that doesn't have to come in through the eyes, ears, nose or skin. You use the awareness of your I Am and your Master Wisdom to sense these things."

"Those are the senses animals use as the most natural thing!"

"The sense of dirt, water and air keeps you in balance."

"Every living being needs these things, from the simplest organism to the most complex one."

"You use your senses to perceive your reality. If you only use the artificial senses, you get a limited perception and therefore live in a limited reality."

This is very exciting for me to hear.

The mind has taken over the original senses that can work over long distances because it works with awareness. The mind has replaced them with senses close to itself, the brain, which must have some kind of physical contact to the subjects it has to detect.

Saint Germain continues, "As I said, the mind/brain doesn't perceive the real human senses. You must be aware in the I Exist, as a focal point. Translated to human words, 'I Exist' is the true feeling you have as you feel yourself being alive; the true Now Moment. The real human senses make life more vibrant and expanding. They add depth to the basic human senses of sight, hearing, smell, taste and feel."

"In the list of senses you gave me a little way back, there is the sense of love. If love is a sense, one can't 'exchange' it between two people."

"Love is a sense, not something you give or receive, but you can experience it together, each in its own way."

"I can share an experience with someone, like Julia and I meeting a beautiful cat, but sensing it is a personal experience for each of us."

Those "new" senses make such perfect sense. This is the only way a tiny new organism could get a foothold and grow. I sense Saint Germain is eager to continue so I send a "continue" to him.

"The sense of focus is one sense, like looking through a clear diamond getting different pictures, representing the artificial senses from each facet of the diamond. This focus will create gravity to the soul in this one sense when time/space passes through the focus. Intelligence results from this focus."

"I guess I must allow these senses to emerge into my human life to expand my awareness. How is this different from communing?"

"Communing is the whole package, so to speak, while the true human senses are the original, basic senses for life to expand and flourish on the planet."

"I assume I can continue to use the artificial senses, but they may be difficult to subdue to give way to the rest."

"When you loosen up the sense of focus to let the other 'divine' senses come in as well, the human senses will not overwhelm you, because the focal point will be less dense, so it doesn't 'blind' you."

"I have a question for you, Saint Germain. Since consciousness is 'outside' time/space, it makes no sense to talk about movement or motion because there is nowhere to move to, right?"

"You're right, Luzi. Movement without motions is expansion/unfolding without a space. This is not for the mind to grasp."

Julia and I reach the gate to our back garden and we say goodbye to Saint Germain. When we come into the garden, we see that Ju-long is already home from work.

He approaches us with open arms. "Oh, here you are. I was just about to text you."

"You're early. You can take your daughter out of the sling. She has been quite joyful today and had her first laugh when a cat struck her face with its furry tail."

"So, it was a furry tail and not a fairy tale! Come to Dad!"

We walk over to the lawn and I place a nice blanket for us to sit on. It is good to sit down, resting my back after the walk back across the fields with Julia in the sling. It gives a different strain to the back than when I carried her inside me. Ju-long plays with his daughter, but I know that it won't be long before she must have a clean nappy and be off to sleep in the pram. I reach for Ju-long's backpack.

"Have you brought any treats with you back from the world?"

"Well, you can take a look!"

I find drinking yoghurt with peach melba. That must be for me. And some bananas for all of us. Even Julia is still just tasting it. I peel a banana and hand it to Ju-long. It is for Julia. The banana is still too heavy for her to hold, but she does her best while Ju-long helps her. Then I peel another one for Ju-long.

"Feeding the monkeys!"

"Tell me how the day with Julia went!"

I tell about the beautiful cat—well, Sekhmet—and I feel her presence while I speak. Then about Julia in her yellow summer dress and my meeting with Pan. When I come to the part with Saint Germain, Julia wants a clean nappy so Ju-long takes her inside. He will get that part later, when he returns with Julia in the pram. Meanwhile, I munch a banana. A question for Josela comes up, which seems to have nothing to do with current events.

"Why does human folklore tell that Elves live in the mountains and mounts?"

"We are not living in your physical mountains, but in another 'dimension', occupying the same space as the mountains. That way your energies do not disturb ours, because you are outside the mountains."

Isis, Adam and Aliyah

This chapter differ from the other ones in this book. Imagine that I, Luzi, together with Julia and SAM merge to bring you this message. You may sense that one of us is more in the front at times.

It starts as I, Luzi, am sitting in my study upstairs with the windows open to let in the gentle summer breeze. I hear the sparrows tweet in the birds' nests in the wall outside. Ju-long is in his beloved vegetable garden, and Julia is sleeping in her pram close to him. I am on my computer, trying to finish some loose ends on one of my projects, but feel restless and cannot get my thoughts around the work.

"Ease up, Mum! You can't force it. Wait until it flows."

It is Julia, and I sense she is not alone. SAM?

"Yes, hi! You know we have some serious plans, and one of them is about the split between the feminine and the masculine!"

"Is it something you can tell me about?"

"Yes, join with us!"

Our conversation is not in words, but the following is my translation of our small talk.

Isis and Adam

In the coming text, we will use words that do not fit with the consciousness and energies they try to describe. We use these words because there simply are no words for these things. We try to explain something we cannot express in human terms, and some quotation marks may show up to mark some words.

We call the two parts of THEO (THe Eternal One), Isis and Adam, also called the feminine and the masculine energy. It has nothing to do with feminine or masculine, or even energy, but we will use these terms.

The initial properties of Isis are strength and creativity. The initial properties of Adam are supporting and nurturing, which demand a level of control. This may seem contradictory to what we would say today. That is very much why we bring this up.

Saint Germain has told that your soul is experienced with energy. At that time Isis was the guiding force with her creativity and Adam her supporter. Later, when things got more out of hand, her strength brought things further out of balance because they were working to find a solution to the energy problem.

At a point, Isis felt that she could not get any further and asked Adam to take the lead while she drew back. Adam, as supporting and nurturing as he was, took over the responsibility in his devotion to

Isis, promising never to give up. As we know from Saint Germain, he failed. Adam could not return to Isis to tell her that he also had failed, even though he had promised never to give up. This caused a split between the two, and they both felt guilt and shame for their lack of ability to solve the issue.

Later, Isis and Adam came to the Order of the Arc and they followed the souls to Earth. Adam, still in control, had developed issues about never giving up and fear of failing, because he had failed to keep his promise to Isis. He could not let go of his control and over time the world became very masculine with focus on control and never giving up.

At a point in time on the planet, through a man, Adam experienced a new feeling, love for a woman. As we know, love is a sense, and cannot be given to anyone, but Adam told Isis about what he had experienced. Isis understood that it was something quite unique, without knowing what it was, so she left everything to discover this for herself.

As we work outside time/space, we can continue the story. Isis discovers love for self and returns to Adam. Adam teaches Isis to feel love for him; Isis feels love for herself, so that is no big deal. Isis shows Adam love for self is a reality.

The temples of Tian

The temples of Tian were the main research facilities in Atlantis and were about 700 km (440 miles) to the north-east of today's Cuba. Some primary places in Atlantis were Cuba, the southern Caribbean, a place in the Pacific Ocean west of Mexico, Mexico City, as the over administrative centre, and Atlanta, Georgia.

The Atlantis era stretches over 500,000 years, about the last 200,000 years without Lemurian. It is understandable that a lot of different things happened in that period. A standardisation or conformity of the body and the mind took place, but without understanding "spirit". Some bodies were as small as a fly and some as big as a mountain. They were very different in appearance as well, some looking, for example, like fish, and others like dogs, and there were differences in brain capacity. There was a general wish to standardise everything. Some of this was done by manipulating DNA in sperm and egg cells.

Later, there was performed further mind control and people became very mental. This was done by hypnosis, surgical intervention and implants, and head bands, like what later became crowns. Those who received these crowns saw it as a privilege because of their enhanced abilities, but did not know the whole purpose.

Implants were made to get the illusion of pleasure, initially for making it easier to live on Earth: people would focus on the pleasure rather than their "miserable" lives. Towards the end some attempts were made to return to dual-sex bodies from the Lemurian period, but without success. With a dual-sex body, one could self-reproduce.

The original split between Isis and Adam created what we could call a consciousness virus of the feminine/masculine imbalance. In the beginning, the virus had the purpose of bringing the consciousness of Isis and Adam back together, but it got distorted by the imbalance and the other feelings, like guilt and shame.

The split also came into the animals and caused them to divide into females and males. When the Atlanteans tried to make the dual-sex bodies again, it was this virus that prevented them from succeeding.

In the end days of Atlantis, in Tian, over 100,000 of us gathered to re-join Isis and Adam in a group consciousness. We allowed our energies to flow and called this Aliyah, meaning self-love. We did it in the pyramid temple of Aliyah to bring in a new balance, with a focus of self.

As you know, Atlantis still fell, but we have ever since worked change into the world. Finally, the new consciousness renders the new energy and whole new Isis/Adam evolved, even not being Isis and Adam.

SAM steps out of our collective.

"When my I Am, Tobiwa, was incarnated during these times in Atlantis, his name was Mure."

I have another question, because I find the name of the practice in the Aliyah temple sounds like the name of the unicorn, Alea, introduced when we first met.

I sense a smile from the unicorn which confirms that the name she had chosen was no coincidence.

We have been talking about the future, so I ask Julia about looking into the future. I sense she is not happy about the question, like it shouldn't need to be asked.

"The mind can't really understand this past/future thing; well, simply because it really doesn't exist. It is an artificial concept made to comprehend the time/space construct."

I sense a short pause, or, better, a redirection of her focus, and then she continues with a smile and a lot of love. "I remember from my future as Julia, only being a few years old, that Grandad Carl and I are out in the snow. I'm dressed in a white suit. We are sitting on the top of a hill; someone has already laid out the slide path. We hold hands, my right in Carl's left. Now we slide down the hill on our butts. It's so thrilling. I feel Carl's joy, and my thrilling mixes in a beautiful dance of 'I exist'."

I sense into this small scene and tears roll down my face.

Moving to Hastings

Dreams about leaving, about another place to stay, and about different connections have come to me lately. This seems strange because I love our home, the house and the garden, and I must not forget the nature and the surrounding people. Leaving the sea is not an option. I have been living near the sea all my life, except my years in London. In one dream, I lived in an igloo, the round house made of snow! Are we moving to the far north, Alaska or Greenland? There must be another explanation for these dreams, a separation of some sort.

Notice to quit our lovely home

It is Sunday 21 July. The owner of the house, Ms Tate, texts me, asking if we will be home in an hour. There is something we must discuss. I reply that we are at home. It will be around afternoon tea, and Ju-long and Julia have been making rolls. Julia is sitting in her chair on the kitchen table, observing her dad creating the rolls that now fill the house with a wonderful smell. The kitchen timer rings, and Ju-long gets the rolls out of the oven.

Ms Tate is punctual, and the doorbell rings an hour later. I have been feeding Julia and have changed her nappy, while Ju-long has laid the table. We will sit inside, but with all windows open. It is too warm to sit outside, even in the shade. I have Julia on my left arm when I open the door.

Ms Tate is a small woman, a little plump, and with curly grey hair. She wears a light-blue shirt, a white skirt and white sandals with some heels. She has a canvas bag with a folder, which she places next to the chair as she sits down.

The visit comes down to this. The Tates had plans to move to California at some point, but then everything fell in place and it is too good to let the chance slip away. They have two daughters over there, living near to each other, bringing up three kids and one under way. Ms Tate has been looking forward to this, and now they can move to California to their children and grandchildren.

This house is being sold, and the new owners will live here themselves. We have a two-month agreement, so we must be out before 1 October.

Ms Tate explains. "It happened as an impulse while speaking with a friend. He offered to buy the house and, the day before, my husband got an offer on our house; the one we live in."

I am in shock. I'm sure Dad would have bought the house if he had known it was for sale. Well it was not for sale!

Julia raises an etherical eyebrow.

"Why do you think it happened this way? Bad luck?" I sense she sends me a smile. "Don't expect things to be worse, just because they change. You should know that."

"But I really can't see how things can be any better

than they are right now."

Julia is still smiling, now with a wink of the eye. "You lack the imagination?"

"Everything here is perfect. Well, maybe not the distances to work and to Mum, Dad and Anna."

My increasing frustration amuses Julia. And here I was looking for some sweet support.

"Just relax, Mum, everything will be fine. Well, even better than fine. It will be great!"

"Easy for you to say. You're just a baby which we have to take care of."

"Oh, I am much more than just a baby. That you know!"

This dialogue happens in less than a second, so my emotions don't have time to show on the outside. Ju-long is remarkably cool. Later he tells me that he had a dialogue with Julia, as I had.

Ms Tate is not happy about the situation. She has the right to give us notice to quit the house, but she knows how much we love the place, and it is the perfect place to raise Julia. Therefore she was in such a hurry to talk to us.

Ju-long does most of the talking. He expresses our surprise, as well as our understanding for her and her husband's situation, and he talks about their lives taking a new and long-awaited direction.

When we say goodbye to her, she seems more re-laxed about the whole situation and seems confi-dent that my parents will be helpful in planning our new life somewhere else. When the door closes behind Ms Tate, Ju-long and I stand looking at each other, like in: "What just happened?" Now I call Dad and explain the situation. He is calm about the situation.

"Great, then you can move out of that old, moist house. A well-insulated house with efficient venti-lation will be much better for not only Julia, but for all of you."

"But we have to be out within two months!"

"Yes, you have just over two months, so you have two months to find a new place to live, and a few days to move your stuff."

I hear Mum in the background, and now she is on Dad's phone. "Hi, dear. What Dad means, and me too, is that in two months you will live in a new and better place. Isn't that marvellous?"

"I can't bring up that much enthusiasm. I see a lot of work and frustration in the time to come."

Julia sends me an inner picture of herself lying relaxed on a red antique sofa, wearing beautiful clothes in yellow and gold from India.

I get it. "Relax in the process."

She adds, "I'll be there all the way, and I can assure you that it will be beautiful, but you must look for the beauty."

Ju-long comes and gives me a hug. "Hi, Mum and Dad!"

"Hi, Ju-long, and congratulations on your new life, starting today!"

"Well, thanks. It certainly will be a new life."

"Carl and I will look out for new possibilities and contact you as soon as we have something. Is Julia awake? Can I talk to her?"

"She's right here, Mum."

I hold the phone in front of Julia. If I hold it to her ear, she will just try to turn her head towards Mum's voice.

"Hi, Julia, it's Grandma. Are you enjoying yourself?"

Julia tries to grab the phone, but her hands are not grown for that yet. She knows that something is going on in front of her. I keep the phone away from her mouth, so she does not slobber on it.

"She has been playing with one of her dad's rolls, but is now ready for a drink, then a clean nappy and a nap, so you can say goodbye. Thank you for your help, Mum. Give Dad a hug!"

"Bye to you all. Don't worry, Luzi. It'll all work out."

I prepare Julia and lay her to sleep in the cradle in the living room. It is colder here than upstairs. The next step is my computer. Subject: houses for rent in Brighton.

As the computer comes to life, my sister, Anna, calls. She has just talked with our parents and wants to share her sympathy. "Hi, sis. Some great news, ha?"

"I would call it grand, like in gigantic."

"How is Ju-long doing?"

"I think we both need the new situation to sink in, but he seems calm. Julia was with us, having a little talk with each of us. We'll be fine. It's just so new."

"So, what now?"

"I have just turned on the computer to search for a suitable home for us; especially Julia."

Ju-long comes in from his vegetable garden with things for dinner. I tell him it is Anna.

"Say hello from me!"

"Ju-long says hello. He has his hands full of lovely greens for dinner!"

"Lucky you!"

"What are you up to, Anna?"

"Nothing. Absolutely nothing! I have a glass of cold white wine in my hand, and dinner is whatever is in the fridge or freezer. I look forward to starting at university again. This summer holiday feel long this year, and Jo-Ann is with her parents in Denmark. She'll be back on Sunday, I think."

"So, my sister has become lazy and lacks motivation!"

"They are some harsh words. I'm not sure they belong in the English vocabulary. I would write an article about that if I had any energy."

"I love you, Anna. You're the best sister I have!"

"And I happen to be your only sister. Lucky me."

Anna can never be serious for long, and she always ends up making me laugh. That is what I do now, as I imagine her facial expression looking bored to death with no will to move. After a while we end the conversation and Anna promises to keep her eyes open for us.

I walk to Ju-long, who is busy in the kitchen, and wrap my arms around him from behind.

"Two months! Luckily, Anna made me laugh. We'll manage."

"We will."

He turns around while drying his hands on the apron, holds me and kisses me. I decide to put the whole thing away for a while and help Ju-long with the dinner. I really enjoy this and I sense Julia like a pink cloud close to us.

New possibilities

Ju-long has just put the dinner on the dining table in the kitchen when Anna texts me. "Turn on the TV on 7!"

It is a program about some families who have been able to buy a large field just outside Hastings to the east where they will build different kinds of dome houses. They have nicknamed the area Dome Home Village. The field is already laid out in parcels, and they have laid plumbing, water and electricity in the ground. As the TV show progresses, we sense the families' enthusiasm while they talk about their different projects. There are different construction methods and materials, all from straw and hay over wood and steel frames to concrete. They show us sketches and photos of similar buildings, and some look interesting. Towards the end of the show they mention that only one building plot has not got an owner yet, probably because it is the largest and therefore may hold the largest dome.

I look at Ju-long.

"It looks very interesting, but what does it have to do with our situation? We can't build a house and move in in two months!"

Julia shows up in what she calls "Grandpa's chair", in a nice evening dress and her hair set up.

"Do you really think you can FIND the perfect home that is already built?"

"Have you lost your grasp on reality, Julia? We

116

can't design and build a house that fast, especially if it is as special as a dome house!"

"Oh, Mum. You are so much in reality that your focus is limited. You don't have to do all this in two months, but just move into something temporary and wait for the house to follow up. It's much easier to find a temporary place to stay. That wouldn't take much effort, and you can start your search close to the building site. You'd better call Grandpa!"

I can feel her excitement, and before my mind has grasped the complexity and found flaws in Julia's plan, I call Dad. Julia fades away her physical appearance, still with a gentle smile on her lips.

I should have known that "it is no problem" when Dad has heard Julia's plan. He calls his solicitor right away and Dad will be the initial owner of the building plot. He also asks us to contact Dome Home Village to make our intentions known. Ju-long finds the project on the Internet and calls the spokesman right away.

Just as I have finished my first bowl of food while Ju-long is still talking on the phone, Julia calls from her cradle that she feels the need for something to eat as well.

I am sitting at the dinner chair breastfeeding Julia when Ju-long puts down the phone and comes over.

"Things are moving fast. I have arranged with Jacob, the spokesman, that he will be here tomorrow at 3 p.m. and I will be home early from work to be here. He will bring his computer with simulation programs and the actual design program to show us some possibilities, cons and pros with a dome home. I like the opportunity not to build a traditional house. I feel it will be great!"

Ju-long is obviously excited, and I remember the image of Julia lying relaxed on the sofa. Just relax. Ju-long picks up the computer to search for a temporary home where we can stay until our dome home is ready, assuming we get the building lot. We don't know how long it will take to design and build the house. Hopefully, Jacob can help us estimate this. We need this information when we apply for a temporary place to stay.

On a side road to Fairlight Road called Tilekiln Lane in Hastings, Ju-long finds an elderly couple looking for someone to take care of their house while they are visiting family in New Zealand from mid-August to the start of the new year. The best part is that Tilekiln Lane stops in what will become the backyard of our new home. We will be close to the building site!

Ju-long calls them right away and gets Mr Brandon on the phone. They had almost given up on finding someone to look after the house and were prepared to lock it down and hope for the best, having neighbours to keep an eye on the property and cut the grass. They are eager to meet us, so suddenly we are pushed for time. Ju-long can shift tomorrow's work and we will drive to Hastings and visit Brandon around noon. At 3 p.m. we must meet Jacob back in Brighton.

"Why don't you move the meeting with Jacob to Hastings? Then he can show you the place and everything."

I recognise the smell of wild rose, which is the typical smell when Julia is around in spirit.

Ju-long makes another phone call and Jacob is pleased to avoid the trip to Brighton. We will call him after our meeting with Brandon and meet with him.

Plans and counter plans; in the end everything seems to fall into place. I call Dad to tell him about the possible arrangement with Brandon.

"Then you have to move even earlier, and most of your stuff has to be stored since you'll live in a furnished home. You only have to take your personal stuff with you. Call Ms Tate about this new development. The new owner might be happy to move in sooner. Oh, and Jacob may know of a container for your things. It might even be placed at the building site! And a last thing. We got the building site, though the papers haven't been signed yet."

Later, as I lie next to Ju-long in bed trying to still my busy mind, the dream about the igloo and the other things from last night comes up. I tell it to Ju-long.

"Ha, luckily it will not be a house of snow. No wonder you couldn't make head or tail of your dream."

"It shows that my mind cannot bring even the closest possibilities into a meaningful description. In that respect, it is almost useless."

In the morning, Mr Brandon calls Ju-long, inviting us to lunch, which is a nice gesture. It is about 40 miles or 60 km to Hastings, which gives us about a one-hour drive. Julia is lying in her pram's cradle on the back seat, sleeping most of the time. I breastfeed her shortly before we arrive at Mr and Ms Brandon's at Tilekiln Ln, which is a narrow road with trees and houses on both sides. Two cars could not pass each other here. Luckily there is a narrow parking space next to the house we can use.

Mr and Ms Brandon come out to greet us. Mr Brandon is taller than I had expected from an inner picture I have of the couple. He has silvery hair and moustache and a strong but kind face. He wears a light-blue shirt and a pair of long dark-blue trousers, even though it is warm. His wife looks extra small when she stands beside him. She has short, curly, grey hair and wears a blue dress with a belt in the same colour and sandals.

We say hello and I ask for a place to change Julia's nappy. Mr Brandon shows me into the house to a small bedroom next to the bathroom. I can lay Julia on the bed. When Julia is ready, Ju-long carries her while we get to see the house and installations. When we are through, Julia sleeps in the pram cradle next to me now sitting at the dinner table. On a chest of drawers, I see a picture of the man whom I thought was Mr Brandon. He is standing next to Ms Brandon in bright sunlight, being just a little taller than she.

"Who is the gentleman in the picture?"

"Oh, it's my brother, George. He and I were photographed some years ago in Australia. It was in 1985. George lived there at that time, but he died in an accident in 1992."

"I'm sorry to hear that. He seems to have been a kind and loving person."

"Yes. George was always there for me, especially in our younger years. Later, he moved to Australia."

As we are having lunch, it is obvious from their conversation that they have accepted us to take care of their house for the rest of the year. I sense no disturbance in my system and, with a short eye contact with Ju-long, we agree to take this opportunity.

Halfway through a biscuit with cheese, Dad calls to tell that he has signed the papers for the building plot.

"Now you must clear everything about building the dome house, the time plan and the plan for the economy. Sign nothing about the building before I have had some trusted people look it through, even though I have a good feeling about this project."

"It's incredible, Dad. We have the plot, a temporary

house next to the building site and I'm waiting to hear from Ms Tate. We'll meet with Jacob—I don't know his last name—when we leave here. I assume that a loan for buying building materials wouldn't be an issue."

"The money isn't an issue, but we must be sharp on the legal part and the construction part. How is my granddaughter, by the way?"

"Oh, she's so sweet. She slept most of the time we were driving and finished a meal just before we arrived. Now she is sleeping next to me in her pram's cradle. We'll get in touch when we have met with Jacob. Give Mum a hug."

Ju-long and I made this agreement with Brandon: We pay rent as long as we live in the house. If we move out before they come back, we must still visit the house daily to make sure everything is all right. Water leaking is the worst problem, next to fire. We will meet one more time, just before they leave. There is some contact information they must bring up to date.

Ju-long calls Jacob. He is at the site so he will come and meet us. There is a wide wooden gate that opens into the site, so we drive through and park on the other side.

As we step out of the car, a strong man approaches us. He smiles and waves before he takes off his working gloves.

"Hello, I am Jacob Langley or JL or Jail."

He is one of those people you feel confidence about, even though you haven't met them before.

I look around. They have laid out an asphalt road and a pavement. Great, otherwise it would be quite muddy when it rains. Sticks are coming out of the ground everywhere, together with tubes or heavy electrical wires. It looks like total chaos. I see some containers as well. People are coming back from lunch break and heavy machinery is turned on. I pull Julia's pram out of the car because I can hear from the men's talking that we will take a tour before we go to the mobile site-hut to look at the more technical stuff like drawings, schedules, photos and videos.

Julia is awake and seems to feel safe in company with the big man. I pull the pram's top over Julia to keep her out of direct sunlight. As we move from site to site, people wave or come over to say hello. I get the sense that this is a close community where everyone knows everyone. I tell this to Jacob.

"Yes, I feel we are a big family, and we have known each other for a long time. I'll go so far as to say that we are brothers in arms, but that needs more explanation. The project started out because we wanted to explore alternative ways to build houses, both in design and use of materials. We found out we couldn't buy any plot suitable for building a normal house and then build a dome house. It took a lot of hard work and many meetings to end up with an area allowing for dome houses, and finally we got a dispensation. This has to be done because normal building laws could not be applied to this very different way of constructing homes. After this, an actual area had to be found and then all the groundwork must be done, like plumbing, water and electricity."

"So, there is no district heating?" I ask.

"District heating was problematic, because we couldn't guarantee drawing a certain amount of energy per year so the back payment of the construction costs would take too many years and thus be unprofitable. We must heat our homes by other means, and that is fine with us. Rather that than be forced to pay a high price for district heating."

This impresses Ju-long. "It has been quite an achievement to get this project up and running."

"The local authority uses our initiative to promote themselves as innovative, which we to a large degree use to our advantage. You could say that we both benefit from this arrangement. It took some time for them to see the light in the mutual benefit, so to speak. It is actually you who finally makes it possible. The last lot had to be sold before the authority would give permission to build on the site. Most of the lots are small and with small domes to reflect the amount people can pay. By far most of the work we'll do ourselves. Each of us has special skills and knowledge which we share with each project if someone needs it. This depends on how a house is built."

We arrive at the mobile site-hut; the command bunker, as Jacob calls it. The hut has a large canvas poster on the side: "The Dome Home Village. New community in Hastings." Ju-long lifts Julia, still in the cradle, and Jacob holds the door while we walk inside.

There is not much free space, and there are a lot of things I do not know the function of. There is a long table, for meetings I guess, and a computer table with a large screen, a printer and even a plotter. The plotter is a drawing machine that uses pens to draw on large pieces of paper.

Jacob walks through the hut, opening all windows to their full capacity. I guess that the hut is as cold in the winter as it is warm in the summer.

I comment on my observations of the site. "The people have moved quickly, if they got the news of the last lot being sold this morning, and are already working."

"I blew the whistle when we had talked on the phone yesterday and, shortly after, the heavy machinery started to move in. Even though it is summer now, we have a winter coming up."

Ju-long is excited to work on planning our new house. "How can we get started, Jacob?"

"We must consider a lot of options before we can construct a dome house. We used to think of a house as a large rectangular box divided into smaller ones. It is easy for the brain to imagine this box system. The dome house has a circular, or at least a rounded, outline and no straight corners, and 90 degrees vertical outside walls."

This gives me an idea. "One could say that we have to think 'organically' in a way, like how nature would build a house."

Jacob becomes excited and brings some pictures up on the large computer screen. Some show cut-throughs of plants and seed capsules. After some time, we start to look at the two major ways to build a dome house, geodesic and monolithic. Roughly, the geodesic way is by using a lot of triangles to shape a dome. This takes a lot of joints and edges that must be sealed. The monolithic way is to create one large shell and then make cut-outs for windows and doors. The outer surface of the shell or dome must have thorough protection from the weather by coating or other means.

A geodesic dome house.

A monolithic dome house.

The triangles seem to be a lot of fun to play with, but the many connections worry Ju-long. "How does one make the monolithic dome?"

Jacob pulls up another set of photos that shows the method.

"You start by casting a circular slab of concrete over a foundation with a ring beam in the house's diameter. Then you attach an air form to the ring beam and inflates it with air from large fans, which keep running until the shell can stand on its own. Now you work on the inside and spray polyurethane foam on the membrane and attach rebars to it. The inner walls are shown with attachments in the rebars. The next step is to spray a special concrete, called shotcrete, on the rebars and this builds the actual walls. Now you have your basic dome to work with."

"What about the membrane?"

"The membrane will stay inside the construction and works as a moisture barrier."

"It must be extremely dirty work."

"It is, but you are covered in a special suit with helmet, glasses and breathing support."

"I'm sure it will take special skills to do the spraying."

"Yes, but we are helping each other, and the local helpers become new friends. I call it group self-build, where we share experience, expertise and tools as well as the knowledge of dealing with officials and legal issues. Don't worry. You will soon learn to make a rebar and work with different materials and tools, helping others piecing together wall elements. There is a lot of work that does not need special skills other than being handy and using common sense. There are those who don't take part in the construction work. As more and more people move out here, food must be cooked, clothes must be washed and dried, kids must be picked up from kindergarten and school. Yes, and homework. Don't forget this part needs to work as well, and with people to take care of these things, the rest can focus on building the homes."

Now I can really feel into this project, and when Julia comes forth with her enthusiasm, I see the beauty of it all. I sense a lot of presence from many of the nonphysical entities I have got to know over the last few years. Julia's and SAM's smiling faces are right behind the computer screen.

"I told you, Mum. Well, without actually telling it. That is why we HAVE to be a part of this community. Things WILL be much better; better than the good place we now move away from."

I have made my decision about what type of dome house it should be. "I would choose the monolithic method. The photos you have shown remind me a little of the way they build, say, around the Mediterranean, especially Saint Torino. Smooth edges and curves."

Ju-long nods. "Me too, but how large should it

be? It is more difficult to estimate the size of the rooms."

We have a lot of talk back and forth, and I must take care of Julia as well. We end up with a dome with a fifty-foot diameter and find the best spot to place it on the plot. Jacob gives us some floor plans to take home. When we feel we are ready, he will call for a meeting with some head people to make an initial plan for the construction. This plan will be important because we will buy materials with the others, to get a better price, and we must know when we need the things at the different construction sites. Jacob gives us a phone number to someone from whom we can hire a container for our stuff in Brighton.

I have become hungry and so has Ju-long, so, after thanking Jacob for his time and wisdom, we drive to a Chinese fish restaurant near the sea. From here I call Mum and Dad to bring them up to speed. They want to visit us in Brighton tomorrow to offer their input with the floor plan, if they can stay overnight. Of course, they can.

Ms Tate calls to tell us that the new owner can move in as early as 15 August. This will be pretty tight, as we can move into Brandon's the same day. We can have our things out and clean the house by that date.

Ju-long calls the guy with the container and we can have it next week; including large cardboard boxes. We don't have that much stuff in the house in Brighton. The things we will need at the Brandon house we will place at the end, so they are easy to access. Now I see that we have more than enough time and I can relax.

Ju-long drives all the way back to Brighton. We don't talk much in the car, and Julia sleeps all the way, right until Ju-long parks the car. Then she cries and wants a clean nappy. Ju-long bathes her before he returns a clean and hungry baby girl to me for a meal before it is bedtime. Ju-long will tuck her in. He has learned that reading a bedtime story for her is a good way to bring her to rest. I suppose she does not understand the story, but that is not the point here. She gets the pictures through Ju-long.

When he returns from Julia, I am at the low table in the living room with floor plans all over. I am too tired from all the impressions and information so we make tea and a few biscuits with cheese and jam.

Later, when we are in bed, we are very pleased with the day and marvel about the synchronicity of things. Today we have been too busy to call our family in Hong Kong, so we must do it tomorrow.

The next day Mum and Dad arrive so we can have lunch together. As always, they are excited to be with Julia. She is in the lying chair on the dinner table, enjoying the attention.

After lunch, still with food on the table, we gather in front of the computer to call our family members on Hong Kong Island. We start by calling Grandma

Jiang in the retirement home. She is already in the computer room making invitations to a picnic with two of her friends. She is happy to see that we and Julia are well; the thing about moving and building a house is less interesting for her.

I whisper to Dad. "Can we invite Kong and Grandma over for Christmas? Will the house be ready?"

"Yes, we can, and the house will be ready to live in. We will pay for Kong's trip. He will look after Grandma. She can't make the trip alone, but she knows how it works. Maybe Ting and Cheng will travel too, or I may head back from China from a business trip at that time."

Grandma is excited to be able to meet Julia, and she has become acquainted with Kong, Ju-long's dad, through their common social projects for people on the island.

After Grandma, it is Ju-long's mother, Ting, and her husband, Cheng. Especially Cheng is interested in the building project, and we have to stop his many questions by promising to send him materials soon. Ting and Cheng have plans for Christmas, but holidays in late spring may suit them.

Ju-long texts his father, Kong, and, shortly after, we can connect on the computer. After coming out of his solitude condition, he has become active with other people, including projects with Grandma. He has had experiences with Julia in the nonphysical realms, and he would very much like to meet her baby self. He has no experience with flying, but he says that Julia will guide him and he has Grandma's experience as well. Dad says he will make his arrangements too.

After the talks with family, we clean up after lunch while talking about the time to come.

Dad wants to prepare us for the most pressing matters. "The coming days may be hectic because most details about building materials must be in place. Jacob and the others will help you. The technical people will make drawings, and we will select the exact place for the house. I imagine that Ju-long will be more on the site than you, Luzi, but you will feel more in contact with the process when you move to Hastings. We have made a special building account for the project, so there should be no problem paying for materials."

Ju-long wants to be clear on that part. "How does this work with payment when we shop for all the houses?"

"One of Jacob's people has a computer program that deals with all details. Each house has its own file, with materials, prices and money deposited, and there is a common file—'the bunk file' they call it—that lists all the materials. This is the shopping list. When materials are brought to the site, it is added to each house's file according to each house's requirements. You can always see what materials you have and how much you have paid. You register your working hours as well, because you'll not always be working on your own house and others will work on yours."

After lunch, Julia is sleeping and the rest of us

132

gather around the large dinner table with the floor plans. They are all scaled to fifty feet in diameter and on one level. This gives a gross area of 1963 square feet. It may sound like a large house for a small family, but we must subtract areas taken up by windows and doors. Jacob suggests it will be 1770 square feet, and we still have the curved-in walls.

After some debate, we have selected the most suitable floor plan and start more detailed changes.

Mum is the first to comment on the floor plan in front of us. "You walk right into the living room. Imagine dirty boots and wet clothing! There is no back door."

A solution may come from Dad. "There is the laundry room next to the kitchen. You can put a door there, but then you have to make the laundry room larger. To do this, the kitchen must be moved into the dining area and it will collide with the main entrance in the living room."

Ju-long finds a way to get more space in the living room. "There are four bedrooms. We could cancel one and add the space to the living room. Then there is space for adding a small room between the main entrance and the living room, with an extra door. Like and inwards going annex."

We change other things as well, and when we think we have finally got it, Dad speaks out despondently. "A garage! You can't have a box standing next to your round house."

Ju-long pulls out the memory dongle with pictures he had got from Jacob. To make it short, the house comes to look like an igloo with the garage added like the igloo's entrance.

Dad suggests covering the dome with transparent solar electric tiles. He owns part of a company that produces such tiles and he could offer them for a low price because it would be part of a show off for the company, especially because it is a dome house.

Ju-long sees a problem here. "But what about the top of the dome? Tiles wouldn't fit there."

"We'll make a large, slightly curved plate, or one divided in three, that will look like the rest of the tiles. We must add a framework to the outer surface of the dome for the tiles. I will call the chef engineer so he can calculate an estimated price and material count for Jacob. Meanwhile, you can send the floor plan to Jacob, Ju-long."

There are a lot of details I do not present to you, reader, like floor materials, windows and doors, room and water heating, ventilation, electricity and light.

At teatime, we have made the initial decisions and must wait for Jacob to return with the rough timetable for the house's construction and outside areas. Julia wakes up and joins us in the garden, entertaining her grandparents while we have tea. Later, it is time for a walk, and Julia falls asleep in her pram.

Mum and Dad stay overnight as planned, and tomorrow they will visit the building site in Hastings on their way back to Sevenoaks.

Ju-long will have to plan his ordinary work around working on the site in Hastings, but he can't add a lot of working hours until we move to Hastings in about three weeks. Instead he spends his time finishing some projects in both Brighton and London. We will get the container in a week.

During the night, in one of my waking periods, Julia contacts me.

"There is a thing you have to talk to Jacob about. We need a better flow around the Dome Home Village and easier access for us and people who come looking at the site. I will show it to you on a map tomorrow. You must not go mental with this tonight."

Next day, Wednesday, when Julia and I are alone in the house because Ju-long is at work at the university and my parents have left, I call up a map on my computer.

I sense Julia "looking over my shoulder", guiding my sight. The construction site has Fairlight Road to the north and Barley Lane to the south with the entry, the two roads only being connected by a bicycle path.

"It would be relatively easy to connect the two roads at Hasting Country Park. We should widen the last part of Barley for better accessibility. In the winter, there is nowhere to put the snow because of the trees on both sides. We will work on this from our side, and you must bring it into mass consciousness for it to come into motion."

I take a screenshot of the area and e-mail it with a comment to Jacob, asking for his opinion.

Hastings

I move my story to the day after we have moved into Brandon's house in Hastings, where we will stay until we can move into our own round house. It is Friday 16 August, and my sister Anna will stay the weekend to look after Julia while Ju-long and I work at the building site. Tomorrow will be my first real working day as my contribution to the project. Anna has taken the train from London and will arrive soon. There is only a ten-minute drive from the local station, and she will take a taxi.

Hastings is 36 miles, 58 km, east of Brighton. Ju-long will have a little over one hour by train to and from work. Even though the Dome Home Village is on the outskirts of Hastings, we are still close to kindergarten and school, even though it is unlikely we will use it, and shopping facilities like Aldi/B&Q on Old London Road.

Our new address is or will be 111 Barley Lane. There is a small lake nearby, a small forest, fields, and we have less than a mile to the sea. We have easier access to the beach than in Brighton, and a large part of the beach is like the one we know from

Hong Kong Island. It IS better than Brighton, as Julia said.

"I told you, Mum!"

"Yes, you told me, Julia!"

"And now Aunty Anna is at the stairs. I'll be so charming!"

I am halfway up from the sofa when I hear the doorbell.

"Hi, sis!"

"Hi, Anna!"

"And where is Aunty Anna's favourite niece?"

"She is sleeping in the living room, but I guess she'll soon wake up for a meal and clean nappy."

Anna puts down her two large bags and finds her way to the cradle in the small living room.

"Oh, she's awake, lying there smiling! She is reaching out for me; see?"

Anna reaches down and takes Julia up. I know it won't be long before I must take her so I make myself comfortable on the sofa. Anna makes her silly baby sounds and Julia laughs. Then my daughter sees me over Anna's shoulder and makes the connection: Mum equals food. She tells Anna with sounds that Aunty has fallen out of favour.

Ju-long and I have trained baby Julia to drink my

milk from a bottle. This will prove useful when I must work at the site while Anna looks after her. Even though I will be close, it might not be so practical that I have to leave in a hurry.

When Julia is fed, Anna makes her ready and puts her in her chair at the dining table near the kitchen so she is part of it now that Anna and I prepare dinner. Ju-long will be here at 8 p.m. Tired, I guess.

Ju-long is back at 7.30 p.m. and takes a shower. He is tired, but starving, he says. Anna does the table and takes the flutes out of the oven, while I feed Julia. Ju-long comes out of the shower and can take over Julia and give her a quick bath in the sink before laying her to sleep in her cradle in the bedroom. Anna and I are sitting at the dinner table when he returns.

"You stopped earlier today?"

"Yes, we were done with what we had planned and there wasn't time to start up a new task."

During dinner, Anna tells us about her life in London.

Anna and I had made a large portion of food so there would be enough for Anna for lunch tomorrow, but it seems that we reach the bottom of the pots.

Ju-long asks around. "Does anyone want more? Anna?"

"No thanks. You just take the rest."

"I thought you weren't able to say no, Anna!"

I know the reason. "She knows there is dessert, 'ice cream!"

"That usually doesn't stop her!"

"I'm just polite, that's all! Now finish up, so we can get the ice crème before it melts!"

After cleaning up, Anna draws a bag of chips out of one of her bags and we play a few rounds of Yahtzee with seven dice. This is an extended version taught to Anna by her friend Jo-Ann. No TV and no movies. Both Ju-long and Anna are tired after a long week, so we go to bed early. I know that I will have a hard day tomorrow and Sunday as well, so it is fine with me. Anna sleeps in a small guest room.

It is Saturday morning at the construction site. First, Ju-long takes me to our plot to show me how far we are with our project. There is a huge round slab of concrete, fifty feet in diameter, with iron rods sticking up all the way around and where the inner walls will be. Pipes for plumbing, water and for the electrical wiring are there. I will not be working at our house this weekend, but at one of the other houses. Today is a big day, and Ju-long will assist with raising the dome to learn the whole procedure. First, they fasten the "balloon" and blow it up with some huge hair dryers. Later he will learn to attach the steel wire grid when the foam is blown at the balloon membrane and make attachment points where the inner walls will attach to the dome. Tomorrow they will add the concrete, the shotcrete, called so because you shoot or spray the special mixture onto the membrane with a pipe on a hose. It will be pretty messy, I can imagine.

We walk to the mobile site-hut to check in for our work assignments. I look forward to finally doing more serious work and to meeting some new people. I feel a little awkward in my working gear, which I usually don't wear.

Ju-long has to leave and I kiss him goodbye. I will work with three other women. Layla is already there. We will assemble a smaller geodesic dome using triangular elements. The other women know each other and the project, so Layla, whose house we will work on, shows me the drawings. It will be a twenty-five-foot dome made of wood and two shells, an outer and an inner, with insulation and ventilation between the two layers.

I have seen that some other houses use large modules of different shapes, but luckily the ones we will be working with at Layla's house are handier for us. We will have a crane outside and a lift inside the dome. The lift must be taken apart when removed from inside the house.

Linda and Lena show up and we leave for the designated plot. It turns out that Layla's house is next to ours and has number 109. It is one of the smallest lots. All the twelve houses or plots have odd numbers, starting with 95. We have already named our little work group The Four L's. Layla is a strong woman in every sense. Her husband is not on the site this weekend, and their two children are at The Kids Group supervised by some other adults. Linda and her husband have four kids. She has fair skin and medium-blond hair in a pigtail. She is a little heavy, but it is not all fat, which I realise when we start working. Lena is not as tall as I and has a robust body and long, curly brown hair. She is very connected to the earth and has plans to grow organic crops on a larger scale with some other people. This may interest Ju-long.

Layla explains the materials and tools before we start. The first row of triangles has been firmly attached to a short wood wall attached to the foundation to get some initial height and an upright wall. Now it is relatively easy for us to build onto them with little measuring. Even though the house is only half the diameter of ours, it is still large when you look down from the platform or the crane. The wall slowly gets higher, but it takes time because we have to fasten the insulation and ensure that there is space for ventilation between it and the outer shell. The covering at the windows must be made individually. There will be two windows up high in the construction which can open with a special mechanism, but we won't get that far today.

Later in the morning we have a tea break. Two young boys come with tea and sandwiches. They are too old for the Kids Group, but to give them some useful activities and some pocket money, they are given the job of serving the kitchen group.

Layla greets them. "Hello, boys. What a wonderful job you have. Do you realise that you make many people happy by bringing what they need?"

Linda adds her compliment too. "Your job is of great importance. If every building group had to go to the kitchen and make their own food, eat, clean up and walk back to work, a lot of time would be wasted."

Lena continues the praise so the boys can't feel less than heroes. "Your work may give each building worker an extra hour, and when you add that up, the village will finish earlier."

I take a little different approach with my comment. "I think we can all move in before Christmas. Wouldn't that be lovely?"

When the boys have left and we sit enjoying the break, I sense the presence of Alea, the unicorn.

"I sense you are happy with the way things turned out, even though we had to kick you out of your old house."

"Yes, everything has been working out beautifully from the start, even though I was anxious in the beginning. Our lives will be so much better; or richer may be a better word to use. We will live amongst people who we can relate to. This village will definitely make a difference to the whole area."

"Yes, Luzi. To have Julia here to 'ground' the highest awareness for people to connect to in this area is very useful. Everyone here will make such a difference because things are brought out in the physical through their thoughts and actions."

Lena turns towards me. "I sense the presence of some of the entities in this area."

I try to explain. "I think they are grateful for our contribution to the overall expansion of consciousness through our thoughts and actions."

Linda is passionate about the possibilities for change. "There is a lot to work on. Education, all from kindergarten and up, and health through healthcare and food. Well, new ideas to do things differently."

Lena feels positive about the "common" people in and around Hastings. "I think people will take in the ideas. We just need to present it for them, not only in words but in action. We must show them how things can be done differently."

In my inner conversation, I pose a question to Alea. "Why couldn't we—I mean Julia, Ju-long and I— have done the same in Brighton?"

"In a sense, you or we could, but one answer could be that it was easier to move you to Hastings than bring everything to Brighton. But, again, that is just one answer."

Julia, who is such a big part of it all, joins in. "I want us to have a NEW house. A house that no one has lived in. I want you and Ju-long to have more opportunities, as you will see later. You will find that what has come up in this short talk amongst the four Ls touches strings that will resonate and bring more energy in."

I have to state a point. "A little cryptic, isn't it?"

Julia smiles. "I told YOU everything and your mind nothing."

I will jump the story to the next day, Sunday, where we will end our working day early, about 4 p.m.

Anna texts me and Ju-long close to 4 p.m. "Julia and I would like to invite her mum and dad to meet them at the New Hong Kong Kitchen, 211 Harold Rd. We will dine at the water reservoirs close by. You can take the car and park at the reservoirs."

I coordinate with Ju-long. After a quick shower at the house, we drive to the reservoirs where we park on a small strip of grass. We walk to the New Hong Kong Kitchen, which is a tiny takeaway. Anna and Julia wait outside. Julia wants to be with me, having her breastfeed, so I sit on a low ledge with her. Anna hands Ju-long and I each a menu card. After we have chosen what we want, Ju-long and Anna go inside to order, while I enjoy some peaceful moments with my daughter in the sun.

When Ju-long and Anna come out with our food, we head for the reservoirs with Julia in the push-chair and Anna driving.

The reservoirs are the Clave Vale Angling Club reservoirs, being two small lakes next to the back-yards of the houses to the east of Harold Rd. The northern lake touches up to a narrow strip of trees, and the southern lake has some vegetable gardens on the eastern bank. Bourne Stream, coming from the north, feeds the lake with water.

There are some benches where we sit and enjoy our food. The food is good, made from fresh materials! Julia wants to sit with her father, so he picks up some blankets from the car and puts them on the grass. Now we can all sit here, and Julia is lying between Ju-long and I. We spend a lovely time here. Later, we pick up Anna's things at the house and I drive her to the station while Ju-long gives Julia a bath.

It has been a hard but rewarding weekend, and we have accomplished quite a bit. Our dome house must have a week for the concrete shell to harden. It will take much longer to harden all the way through, but after a week they can build the inner walls and place tubes for the electric wiring in the walls. The garage, which also contains a room for garden tools and a room for our bikes, must be constructed differently, because it looks more like a tunnel or archway.

Julia's first babysitter

Ju-long and I have got many new friends and connections since we have moved to Hastings, in particular through people connected to the Dome Home Village. We have been able to select a babysitter for Julia; with Julia's approval, of course. This is how it came to be.

One late morning I am just about to hang out washed bed linen to dry with a plan of visiting the construction site with Julia in the pushchair afterwards. I smell Julia's scent, wild rose, when she contacts me.

"You should leave the clothes until later and walk to the site right away."

"But the clothes may be damaged if I leave them here, all curled up and wet."

"Place it in the cellar and put baby Julia's bathtub upside down over it. Then it'll be OK!"

I do what Julia asks and, shortly after, we are on our way.

"Why such a hurry? Is there something wrong?"

"Not at all. Everything is fine. You'll see!"

I find Ju-long working with Jacob and his wife. They are helping to set up a dome home of six small domes connected, one in the middle and five placed around it. A young girl in her mid-teens comes out and is about to leave. I say hello to everyone, and the girl is the first to come over.

"Hi, I'm Sarah."

She is not tall, with a slim body, wearing a white T-shirt with a monarch butterfly, blue jeans shorts and white sneakers. She has fixed her long, brown, slightly curly hair on the top of her head because of the mid-August warm weather.

"Hello, Sarah. I'm Luzi and this is Julia. She is three and a half months. Ju-long is her father."

Sarah squats beside the pushchair. "She is so adorable!"

I sense Julia smiles. "Sarah is my first babysitter; she just doesn't know it yet!"

"You sound pretty sure."

"Oh, yes!"

The others come over and Ju-long kisses Julia and then me.

Jacob's wife, Iona, comes next. "This is our daughter Sarah; she's seventeen and our eldest. If you ever need a babysitter, I can recommend her. She has experience with her younger siblings and has had sitter jobs as well."

Sarah gets up and is excited. "I would love to take care of Julia. I feel she is gentle and easy to be with."

"But Julia is still very young. She has only been with

my younger sister Anna, and she is twenty-five."

I sense Julia is shaking her head. "I told you, she's my first babysitter, and it will be fine!"

Sarah brings out her arguments. "Don't worry, Luzi. I am good with babies. I work at a kindergarten. They have kids from six weeks, even though it is not common."

Ju-long asks her a question she might be tired of answering. "Do you have any plans for your future?"

"I'll be eighteen before I start at the East Sussex College at *Level 4/5 foundation degree in early years*. You must be at least eighteen to attend and have a normal HE, as well as a relevant workplace for twelve hours per week and the workplace's assistance."

HE means higher education, which has certain requirements.

Jacob has joined us. "She'll use her connection with Artemis Nursery and they have made an agreement."

Sarah elaborates on her coming education. "It is a two-year course and I'll start in October."

I comment on her two years at college. "I guess you could use some money to put aside before you start. If you could look after Julia some days, I could contribute with some working hours here at the site."

"I would be very happy to take care of Julia and

wouldn't mind starting right away!"

"I have some wet laundry to hang to dry outside, so I must go back. You can come with Julia and me so we can talk. I will not work on the site today. I have some writing to do. Ju-long, we can talk when you come home."

I can see he is a little confused about why I must leave right away, but he nods.

Sarah and I have a good talk while walking around the site before returning to the rented house in Tile-kiln Lane. I get more relaxed about her capabilities for handling Julia. Now I just need to see her in action. We go straight to the laundry in the cellar and Sarah gives a hand at the clothes line. Julia cries and we sit in the chairs in the garden while I breastfeed her. Julia is not particular hungry and soon cries again. Sarah changes Julia's nappy and lays her to sleep in her cradle indoors. It is too hot outside, but we keep the windows open to give her fresh air. I am no longer in doubt that Sarah can handle baby Julia, just as Julia said. Now I am interested in how close their relationship will be.

I take some of Ju-long's homemade ice tea from the refrigerator and we sit down just outside the open window so we can hear if Julia calls. I decide to go for it and start the talk. "Your family is open to new ideas, so I will share the first moments I met Julia."

I tell how Julia's name came to me before she was born, and how Ju-long and I met her being a young woman outside normal human awareness.

Sarah is excited. "It's so cool. I knew Julia is special. I have already met her."

I am surprised, because Julia had not told me anything. Now I understand why she was so sure about Sarah.

"Is it something you would like to share with me?"

"It would delight me."

Here comes Sarah's story.

"I guess that some initial thought I had about my future triggered the event. I had decided to work with young children, because so many are born with a higher awareness of themselves and why they chose to be born. This way I can support them in a world that is less aware of their situation. I think it is part of starting this whole community with the Dome Home Village and all that will follow.

"One night I wake up after having an experience that was more real than a dream. This is what happened. I step out of my home and see a beautiful young woman with a pushchair in which she has her baby daughter. At first, I feel a little strange, because I know that the woman and the baby are the same person. We communicate without using our voices.

"'Hello, Sarah, you can call me Julia, and this is baby Julia, who is me as well.'

"The young woman has slightly Asian facial features and her long hair is lighter than mine. She wears a beautiful dress above the knees in the same colours as the wild rose, pink gradually changing to be indigo at the bottom. Her scent is of wild rose as well.

"We are in a beautiful meadow with a lot of flowers and I sit down next to the pushchair. It is a beautiful baby girl with teeming green-blue eyes.

"'You can pick me up. I want to feel the grass and the flowers under my feet.'

"I pick her up, and, while still holding her under her arms, I carefully place her feet on the grass. She starts to kick in joy and laugh out loud.

"Adult Julia sits next to us with a gentle smile and the same wonderful eyes looking at us. 'This is how you will act in the world. Bringing joy, self-respect and understanding to those that feel that they have made a wrong choice by coming here, or simply need someone who can understand their situation.

"Baby Julia wants more experience. 'You can let go of me now.'

"She bumps down, sitting on her bum. She grasps grass and flowers in her tiny hands and laughs out loud.

"'I am not one of those kids that need this special care, but I will share ME, my wisdom with you, and in that sense, you will never lack wisdom in your work or doubt your actions.'

"Adult Julia hands me a glass of sparkling pink wine. 'My friend Josela is famous for her wine, so I decided to make my own brand, Elvendale Pink.'

"The glass is chilly. First, I smell the wine. The bubbles hit my nose as I bring the glass closer; wild rose. I take a sip; wild rose. The taste is not too sweet and is very close to the smell. The sense in my mouth is chilly and fizzy, but less than ordinary Champagne. I must have touched the rim of the glass with a finger, because it made a sound; well, a small melody. And when I look closer, I see the wine making a swirl, like a dance in the glass, and shooting out beams of fireworks without any bangs or sound. I must take another sip and congratulate Julia on her creation.

"'This wine is … well, really indescribable in human words. It touches more than the human senses.'

"'Indeed. You can sense it because you are not a human while you are here. You are consciousness.'

"'What is this place, anyway?'

"'Elvendale, where we meet with our friends, the Sidhe, whom you might call Elves. Please close your eyes, and I will show you something.'

"I close my eyes.

"'With your eyes closed, please tell me what clothes you wear.'

"'Well, I don't know. T-shirt and jeans, I suppose?'

"'I will ask you to imagine some clothes you don't own. And don't be shy.'

"I had to think a little about that. I mostly wear jeans and a shirt of some kind.

"'Hmm. A dress like yours in shape, but with a pattern like a very large, clear diamond reflecting the sunlight in many colours!'

"I sense Julia approve my choice.

"'Great! That is a dress you wouldn't even wear at a New Year's party! Now open your eyes and look.'

"I open my eyes and get up.

"'Wow. This is so cool!'

"The dress is just as I had imagined. The facets even change in colours as I turn my body.

"Julia explains. 'You do not bring your physical body here, only the imprint, the code if you like. You could choose to appear in a different body, if any, or an animal.'

"I admire my dress and then I have a question. 'Julia, will I remember anything of this?'

"'Yes. It has made such an imprint, and it is not totally weird, so your mind is able to make sense of it. Even if you don't, meeting a woman with a push-chair will trigger a response in you.'

"'Thanks, Julia. I am sure we will meet again like

this, and I look forward to doing so. I hope I'll write this event down, when my consciousness returns to the 3D world.'

"Julia laughs. 'If you don't wake up, I'll tickle you until you do.'

"Now my view swirls into black, like it was the surface of water circling down the drain. When I wake up in my bed, I still have the scent of wild rose in my nose. I sniff in again, but it is gone. I pick up my notebook and write."

Sarah is excited about the experience, and I see that she is happy to share it with someone who knows experiences like hers first-hand.

I would like to attend a seminar at the university in London that cannot be done over the Internet. Now I have Sarah it will be easy without Ju-long needing to stay with her. Today and tomorrow I have work to do on my computer, some of it for the seminar in London. We do not need Sarah until Friday and Saturday, when I am scheduled to work on the site. Sunday, Ju-long and I take a day off with Julia, and Monday I must make the last things for the seminar on Tuesday.

Sarah sneaks in to say goodbye to Julia, and, soon after, she returns and whispers, "She is sleeping and so cute, lying there! I look forward to Friday."

I show her out and then start on my work.

During the day, I enjoy the breaks I have with Julia. In the afternoon I take her in the pushchair to Fishponds Gill, a small stream to the south of Barley Lane, which leads to Ecclesbourne Reservoir. It is all encircled by trees, which gives us the illusion of being in a forest. We spend time at the reservoir where some ducks show up to check if we have brought some bread; and we have. Julia loves being in nature.

Ju-long comes home, awfully dirty, and takes a shower. His work clothes go into the washing machine. He spends time with Julia while I prepare dinner. I double up on the portions, because the manual labour gives Ju-long quite an appetite.

In the evening we watch the movie *Cirque du Soleil: Worlds Away* in the fantasy genre from 2012. It is a fantastic performance and very beautiful and rich in colours, especially watched in 3D on a large TV set.

The next chapter

A day in London

There were some loose plans of having my close friend Cassandra, her boyfriend, Karl, and their baby boy, Walter, who is a few months older than Julia, visit us in Brighton, but then we had to move, so we postponed the arrangement. We have been video chatting instead. This is not the same as meeting with Cassandra in London at *Chao!*, drinking chai latte and eating bagels as we did before both of us had our first baby. With Sarah and the seminar, I can meet Cassandra again.

Even though it is with short notice, I am able not only to attend the seminar, but also have been given time to make a presentation on one of my topics. I also arrange to meet Cassandra and baby Walter in the late afternoon after the seminar and will call her when I know when I can be at *Chao!*, because one can never know with seminars.

Today it is Tuesday 27 August, and I am going to London. I hear Sarah coming up the stairs, and the clock shows 7.11 a.m. I am sitting in the living room giving Julia her morning feed. Ju-long left to be at the site at 7 a.m.; they will continue their work with the inner walls in our house. Sarah puts down her backpack without making a sound and walks quietly over to Julia and me. Julia grabs and holds Sarah's finger while still suckling. She knows she will be with Sarah today. I am so happy that Sarah showed up last week, just as we needed her. Shortly after, I can hand Julia over to Sarah.

I take my bike to the train station, having all my stuff in my backpack. It is more relaxing to go by train than driving myself. It takes one and a half hours, and I must change trains in Ashford. There are only eight stops in total.

The seminar is interesting, and I get a new view on some subjects. My presentation went well, and I got compliments afterwards.

Before I put away my notes at the end of the seminar, I text Cassandra to tell her I will be at the café in fifteen minutes. I say goodbye to people I know on my way out of the auditorium and head for a side exit. It is raining and the light from the sky has a special glow to it.

It is late, 5 p.m., when I step into café *Chao!* I see Cassandra and Karl and walk over and give them both a hug. Their boy sleeps in the pushchair. I turn to Karl as I take a seat, placing my backpack next to the pushchair. "So, you also have the time to come, Karl."

"Yes. Most days I am home at this hour, and I haven't seen you for quite some time now. You look gorgeous as always, but a little tired I suppose."

"It has been quite a day, but a good one anyway."

Cassandra grabs the menu. "Let's order. I'm starving!" She puts it down again. "I know what I want! Spaghetti!"

Karl wants pizza, and I pick baked pasta and a large chai latte. Karl wants mineral water.

"How is your small family? And you have got a babysitter, I hear."

"My family is fine. Ju-long works at the construction site and works up quite an appetite, but will be at the university next week. Julia is sweet and happy, and loves the first babysitter, Sarah. I'll tell you a little story how it came to be, but tell me first how you are doing."

A few years back, when I started this new life of awareness, I was very much in doubt if I should tell Cassandra about my experiences, afraid that it would push her away. After all, she was, and still is, my best friend. Then I realised that I must stay true, because it would be the hiding that would push her away. She took a little time to get used to the thought and my strange stories, but slowly she accepted that this was part of my life.

Cassandra starts out. "It has been a great summer, for the most part, but, as you know, I had been a little nervous about whether Walter got enough fluids."

Karl laughs. "He pees gallons, so that's surely no problem!"

It has been quite a while since I have seen Walter in

person. "I hope I'll get a chance to hold him before we part."

Karl is proud of his son. "Walter eats solid foods. It seems to be a great experience for him, even though it is still tiny pieces and one at a time."

Cassandra shows a worried face. "I am a little nervous when he will go to the nursery; the food, nappy change, washing, infections."

I have no experiences, just common sense and Julia in the wings. She assures me that Walter will be fine, so I am confident to present my comment.

"I am sure they will do their best. It is in their own interest. Be sure to take time to have a good dialogue with the staff. Show them that you have confidence in them and comment on the good things they do. The infections are a good thing, because they strengthen the immune system, and you can see if the skin is red."

"We have a place for Walter, recommended by one of my colleagues, who has a son there."

"That's great. Then there are more eyes on the place, and you can keep an eye on each other's kids."

Before Cassandra has finished her spaghetti, Walter wakes up and gives a cry. Karl picks him up and talks a little to him. Then he hands his son over to me.

"He is heavy compared to Julia. Of course, he had a higher birth weight and is two months older."

160

I bet Walter will be a mini Karl soon. His eyes, which are brown, look more like Cassandra's though. He cries a little. He wants FOOD! Karl takes him over and gives him a bottle of Cassandra's milk. She smiles.

"I can never run too much milk in my breasts. This glutton makes sure it will never happen. Now and then we give him some substitute, which he takes, but he prefers the real stuff, that's for sure."

We have a good time, and I am glad to see they are doing fine. But, with an hour between trains to Hastings at this time of day, we must part.

At the train I call Sarah to hear how the afternoon has gone.

"We had a great time. Julia is quite active during tummy time, doing some push-ups, and she surely works a lot to strengthen her legs when we 'dance'. I had time to read, so she has been sleeping too."

Ju-long had worked late today, knowing I would be home late. He was back at 8 p.m., and Sarah went home after he had taken a shower. He sits at his computer, but turns it off now that I come in. "Welcome back, love. Tea and biscuits?"

"Hi. Just tea, please. How was your day at the site?"

"Long and hard, but next week we—well, they— will move on with the wooden floor and the water heating under it. I'm sure we will move in long before Christmas."

"Yes, you are not working at the site next week. Lucky you! I have to take my turn, though. I hope I can spend at least some time making our floor to see how it is done. It gives a much better understanding of the house."

I kiss him before I go to the bathroom. When I come back, we sit on the sofa, me curling up in Ju-long's lap, sensing into our wonderful life. We both sense Julia with us.

Another man in the family

It is very early morning and the digital clock shows 2.02 a.m. I feel tired and awake at the same time and I can't sleep anymore. Moving to Hastings, with all the many changes, makes me realise I am starting on a new chapter in my life. I contact Julia to hear what she has to say about the whole thing.

"I can't sleep, so we might as well have a little chat about the future."

Julia drops a bomb. "I look forward to seeing my younger brother in this world!"

NOW I am awake and sit up in the bed. "What?!"

"You are not becoming younger, and we need another man in the family."

"But I am just getting used to one small child. I can't handle two, even if they are sweet and well behaved."

"Not right NOW, Mum, but in a year; max two."

"Why do we need another man in the family?"

"I shouldn't have said the last part, but I'm just so excited. I'm outside time, you know, so I have a different perspective."

"Then, why can't I see these different perspectives?"

"Do you REALLY want to know? And they are still just possibilities."

"Well, I guess not. But you do! How is that different from me?"

"Let's say that I kind of have a summary of the possibilities, but it is not where I have my focus. Let's say that I lay out some tracks that are more like rubber bands, very flexible."

I may as well get up. I am not scheduled to work on the site today, so I can take a nap later, if needed. Ju-long will be up early; they are working on the internal walls on our dome home.

As Julia and I have talked earlier about making the area more accessible, I meet with Jacob in the mobile site-hut at the construction site, having Julia in the pushchair, but pick her up as she whimpers a little. Shortly after, she is smiling at Jacob.

"What an adorable kid."

Much to my surprise, Julia speaks through me. "You may hold her."

I hand her over.

"Oh thanks, I would love to!"

I communicate to Julia. "So, you are really working your charm for this project."

"Ah, Mum, Jacob is not the man we have to convince, but we need his weight to bring things forth. I'm sitting here because we enjoy each other's company."

I bring forth our suggestion and arguments, and Jacob, who knows the area better than I, surely can see the benefits of widening part of Barley Lane and connecting it to Fairlight Road.

Still sitting with Julia, Jacob brings forth his thoughts on the project. "Improving the roads was not part of making the site available to us, so, in that respect, I don't know the plans. There has to be money for the project too and all the preparation. What seems to be a small project may be large or complicated. By complicated, I don't necessarily mean difficult."

I feel less hopeful after this. "Now it seems almost hopeless to go on with this."

"Hey, Mum, you just lack confidence and imagination in what you see as impossible or extremely difficult to bring through. I don't want to tell you to trust me, because it has nothing to do with trust, except in yourself."

Jacob is more optimistic. Thanks for that.

"Your observations are right and your arguments are good. The technicians and I will make some sketches and bring it to an initial meeting with the East Sussex County Council as soon as possible."

He gets up. "Hey, can I keep her?"

"Nope! You must stick to your own kids!"

He smiles and hands me Julia. "You'll hear from me, and thank you for your input. I think it is brilliant. We had too much focus on the actual site to see the bigger picture."

As Julia and I are back, sitting in the garden of our rented house in Tilekiln Lane, I catch the distinct smell of the Sidhe woman, Josela, and sense an invitation to meet in Elvendale.

The large clearing used as a meeting ground in Elvendale emerges, and Julia and I flow to the centre where Josela, the unicorn Alea and the two dragons Loong and Shaumbra sit. Julia appears as the young woman I used to see when we connected outside 3D. We all send our greetings: "Oh-Be-Ahn!"

It is the Merlin greeting meaning: I honour you for the journey, no matter where you are.

The two dragons encircle the rest of the group and it is nice to have something to lean up against. The Unicorn Alea has placed herself where the two dragons' tails overlap. Josela sits with Alea. I choose the white, fluffy-haired Loong, and Julia sits on the leathery crimson dragon's hind leg and uses its belly as a backrest. Josela wears a reddish-brown long dress with a lighter red embroidered ornamentation. It looks like silk because it reflects the sunlight. Her hair is in a plait down her back. Julia wears a short-sleeved light-green dress with pale-yellow ornamentation and blue borders. She wears her hair loose. I wear a mint-coloured dress with a few white flowers at the bottom.

My knowingness tells me that it is an initial meeting about the new community outside Hastings. When I look through the grass and the ground, I can vaguely see the area, as in a bird's-eye view.

There is no chairman, but Julia is the first to speak up. "The ground we take into use is of old times, so it has been occupied and tended for eons by the little people in conjunction with the nature spirits. The consciousness in the area reaches out into the sea, reaching the big river that still flows there. We are attuning this area to its highest potential, because there are further plans for the area than dome houses. There will be established fields to the east for the settlers to use, and the local farmers will change their ways to bring harmony to their crops and livestock. The fishing grounds, both in the lakes and part of the Channel, will improve as well."

Alea takes over. "When the consciousness of the area expands, the local people and even people in a large area, including London, will pick it up and slowly make it theirs. Even though consciousness can't be quantified, its attributes are special for a specific area because it is part of the physical. You can't take a drawing compass and draw a circle, with Hastings in the centre to set its borders, though."

Josela is the next speaker. "When people move their focus from survival and hauling into being aware of their surroundings, they may open to what SAM calls communing, being in dialogue with everything around them. This openness might bring them to see their brothers and sisters of the Sidhe who live as non-physical humans in the same land."

Loong, the white dragon, follows. "This is so much more than a few round houses occupied by a bunch of weird people. As the consciousness we call Gaia withdraws from the planet, people must take over the management. The best or, should I say, most beneficial way is to connect with Sidhe. All manifestations occur in the non-physical realms first."

I have a question important for me to get an answer to. "How much should I tell the people in the Dome Home Village?"

Shaumbra the crimson dragon answers. "Though these people have an open mind to new thoughts and understandings, they are still on different levels of awareness. You'll know what to relay to a person, just as you always have. When you know their interests or passion, you know where they are most open. Use that as a starting point."

Josela loosens up the energies. "I say it is time for a toast to this first new seeding in this old land."

She brings forth a bottle and glasses and continues, "And it has come to my knowledge that another is trying to beat me in the winemaking. Isn't that right, Julia?"

Julia smiles and pulls out a bottle of her wild rose wine. "I didn't know there was a contest. Then I would have put more effort into it!"

Now we are sipping a yellowish wine and a light rose.

The reader might think dragons and unicorns can't hold a glass and drink wine or even use a straw, but here you lack imagination. First, they are not dragons and unicorns, nor are we humans and Sid-he, and, second, none of us need to lift a glass or pour wine into the mouth. We use our true senses to have any experience with drinking the wine. We do not even need the wine!

In the evening I update Ju-long on the day's events. It surprises him that a son is already waiting in the wings. I can tell by his voice and acting that he looks forward to welcoming a son to the family. The road project makes him wonder if it will bear fruit. Ju-long gets very excited to hear about the vast impact the people and the village will have on the whole region.

Baby Julia has a surprise for him as well. In the morning, after Ju-long has left early for work, I discovered that Julia has four front teeth, where two have broken through in the lower jaw, and the two in the upper jaw are clearly showing.

The seed germs

We are in the first week of September. Ju-long is working at the university in Brighton all weekdays.

I have been working at my computer and at the construction site, but today Jacob has invited me to accompany him to a meeting at the county council about the road issue.

Sarah is with Julia, and Jacob picks me up. It is only he and I from the village, and I ask him why none of the technical people are with us. He gives me a wise answer.

"If we show up with more, we could appear invasive, and the people will be in defence. This might seem about technical stuff, but it is about emotions and gut feelings."

Jacob surprises me. He is much more than just a big, jovial handyman. Now I know that Ju-long and I must meet him and his wife and talk about what I have learned in Elvendale.

Soon we arrive and are led to a small meeting room, where three people are waiting, all men. We might only be five people in the room, but I sense so much more, and the "energy" is high.

I will cut the story about the meeting short. They have looked at our papers and spent some time talking about all the things that will make such a plan difficult to bring to life. Now Julia and I go into a kind of meld and add a different and positive perspective to it, including the technical stuff using Jacob as confirmation. During this, I ask Julia how she knows all this stuff and she applies a logical answer.

"I just use their own knowledge and combine it with how I see things are brought to life."

"So, my daughter will not need to go to school, but must just show up at the exams and tell the teacher what she or he already knows."

"Let us talk about these things later. She isn't even in nursery yet."

The meeting does not end up in anything concrete, but I feel that the seed we put in the ground in Elvendale has germinated.

After the meeting, outside the building, Jacob seems as if he is not sure what has happened at the meeting.

"I don't feel I added anything. I was just sitting there, sipping tea while you ran the whole show."

This will be as good a time as any to get closer to the truth.

"Jacob, you have seen how special Julia is. She and I communicate, but not with her as a child. It was she who choose Sarah to be baby Julia's babysitter. Julia is the driving force in all this. She even got us to move from Brighton to support your goal here. It was she who asked to sit with you at the meeting in the mobile site-hut the other day."

Jacob is silent for a moment. Then he smiles. "I knew there was more to that little thing. Even the way Sarah talks about her shows they have a special relationship."

"Jacob, it is much bigger than even that. I feel we must meet, you, your wife, Iona, Ju-long and I to talk about the situation. I feel we will benefit from bringing you in to these layers."

"We can meet at our place, and Sarah can look after the small ones. Augusta, the youngest, is three."

"I, or is it Julia, sense that soon things will move fast, so we should meet soon."

"We could do it on the weekend. Both you and us will not be at the site."

"Let us aim for Saturday, then, and we'll talk later about the time. I must check it out with Ju-long."

In the evening Ju-long is eager to hear all about the

meeting. He soon laughs. He is sitting with baby Julia on the sofa and she laughs as well.

"You really stir things up here in the south-east, even in London. I know you can't take all the credit, but, nevertheless, Daddy is impressed."

Iona, Jacob's wife, calls me, inviting us for lunch Saturday, and it suits us fine.

Julia's birthday present to us

Today it is Thursday 6 September and Julia's four months birthday. We have just below twenty degrees Celsius, clear skies and almost no wind. It is mid-afternoon, and we are at Ecclesbourne Reservoir, halfway to the Channel from our home. Trees to the water's edge surround the small lake, and baby Julia loves the place. We can use the pushchair all the way, even though the path is not even. Ju-long drives the pushchair and I carry the food and drinks, preventing them from being shaken. There is a blanket hanging on the handles of the pushchair.

We always start by feeding the ducks, and Julia wants them up close. I didn't want that at first, but Julia insists that baby Julia can handle it. Ju-long holds her so she can stand up, or else the ducks will walk up her legs. I help her hold the bread in her stretched palm. She is not the least afraid of them, and they are gentle with her, not invasive at all. She has ensured me that she won't get sick from the contact. The nature spirits of the immediate area always show up when Julia arrives, and I am getting used to inviting them in. We make a small, safe space where we can enjoy all the life, both visible and what is invisible to most people.

Julia communicates to us about celebrating birthdays.

"I always, like in every second, honour my human part, so my human, being four months old, is not more important than any other day or second. I know you do it to honour life, and you do it through baby Julia. She is the conduit connection to all life. It is how I honour her myself."

We enjoy our own sandwiches and have some of Mum's homemade raspberry/peach juice in a thermos bottle.

On our way back, we walk across a small field of grass. Being in the middle of the field, a red fox is coming straight toward us. We stop, and Ju-long and I sit down on each side of the pushchair. This way we hope not to scare the fox by otherwise being tall. It slows down a few yards from us, stops, but then slowly approaches us, looking at Julia and totally ignoring Ju-long and me. Julia assures us it is fine.

"It's all right. The fox can't hurt me. She has two cubs left, herself. Her den is at the steep slope by the Channel."

Julia brings our awareness into a small circle or bubble, and we can sense much more than the physical nature. I can sense the fox on many levels,

both the animal as a normal fox, the fox's awareness and the consciousness that is not a fox, just
as I am not a human. This is the first time Julia has
given us the opportunity to sense so deep. It also
gives us the opportunity to sense much deeper into
ourselves and each other. It is so beautiful. Our
physical parts do nothing, and I know that on the
outside, the meeting only takes a few seconds, like
a short sniff from the fox and she is off. The connection brings much communion, but I can nowhere
near bring it into human words.

As we leave the bubble in which I had felt so expanded, I must take a moment to get used to occupying such a small space again. I look for the fox
and she is about ten yards away from us, walking
in a normal, relaxed pace on the narrow path on
her way to the lake. She doesn't look back.

Ju-long and I are speechless until our minds have
put a tiny part of it into some kind of order.

Ju-long moves the pushchair. "It was like a connection from the centre of the planet to everything
and no-thing, even beyond this universe, which felt
quite small."

I must agree to that. "Even though Hastings and
this planet has no size compared to ALL. I still felt
its great potency. Not because it is Hastings, but
because of what we do here. Thank you, Julia, for
this lovely birthday gift from you to us."

I sense her smiling. "There is no 'to and from' here,
just IS. And there is no size, by the way."

This evening we make an early dinner in the garden, grilling fish and vegetables, even already cooked rice in a small pan. Ju-long adds oils and spices to the rice. I open a bottle of Australian white wine.

Earlier today we had our close Chinese family members on the computer. They are all doing fine, keeping themselves busy. Grandma talked a little about her old body. Her and Ju-long's dad, Kong, very much look forward to visiting us in December.

Meeting at Jacob's

We take the car to visit the Langley family. Julia uses her car seat, and I sit next to her in the rear. She seems very interested in what is going on around her, even though, I must suppose, she is not aware of what is going on outside the car.

I get an immediate response from Julia. "Oh, don't be so sure about that! She senses dirt, water, air, gravity, electricity, magnetics and light with the natural human senses, which are not of the mind. You remember Saint Germain told you about them?"

"Oh, yes. You will ensure that your human part doesn't lose these senses."

"We are, with the help of Sarah, working on her muscular strength and neuro responses. I guess she'll be able to sit up on her own sometime next week or the week after. Her oral muscles work fine, as does her digestive system."

"But she is just four months old!"

"Remember, this body is with no restrictions from ancestor DNA and built with new energy. I must attend a development that doesn't alert the authorities at the regular health checks other than her quick development surprises them."

As we communicate, I fill in Ju-long.

Julia tells me a little more. "We have a small body structure, which helps, and cheated with the double-up of the first teeth, and the next four are not far away. Most of the teeth will be out when we are one year."

"Remarkable how little growing teeth affects her. The other mothers in the birth group report on quite more pain and irritation."

"It was like the birth. Why do it the hard way when we can do it the easy way?! Pain is an illusion in the first place, and signalling the brain about discomfort when the teeth break through wouldn't ease the process. Both I and the body know what is going on. The normal mind with its survival mode would worry about everything that might be a potential threat, but this is a normal process without complications. Even a beginning infection is handled on the spot. Only if the person has to take action does the mind/brain have to be involved."

Ju-long comments on Julia's statement. "The brain has very little to do and is surely not stressed!"

176

Julia answers. "It is kind of the point here! The mind/brain should only be active when it can do something constructive in the situation."

I have to comment on that, also in the light of what Saint Germain has told me. "So, the mind is hugely overrated?"

"The mind takes over all it can lay its hands on, so to speak. It's a control freak! I don't work in that way. You may say that my human mind is running idle most of the time, especially compared to a normal human mind."

I love these talks with Julia. They give Ju-long and me so much insight, both into her life and what we can expect to turn into as we allow our flow of consciousness into a body that slowly adjusts to these new conditions. Now we arrive, and Ju-long finds a parking spot advised by Jacob.

Sarah and Augusta answer the door, and Sarah welcomes us. I expect Augusta to be much interested in the baby girl coming to visit her. I have Julia on the arm and kneel to level up with Augusta.

"Hello, I am Luzi and this is Julia. She will be one year next year. Julia is still a little baby."

Augusta straightens up. I can hear that she and Sarah have been talking about Julia. "Yes, she can't walk. I'll be four at Christmas."

Sarah invites us in. "Let's go inside. Lunch is ready."

Iona and the son, Peter, twelve years old, approaches. Iona turns to Ju-long. "You can put Julia's things there by the counter."

I hand a small wrapped gift of authentic Hong Kong-style milk tea to Iona.

"Oh, thanks. I look forward to seeing what it is."

We have said hello, and Ju-long places Julia's cradle from the pram into a large armchair so she will be more in level when we are sitting at the table. Jacob comes out from the kitchen wearing an apron.

"Oh, there is my little angel. Now I have two!"

The last part is a correct statement to make, as he sees Augusta's expression. I place Julia in the cradle, and Augusta and Jacob gather around. I pull back a little. I breastfed her before we drove off and hope she will doze off soon.

At the table, Ju-long gets a dialogue going with Peter about computer games. Later, Ju-long tells me that Peter is not used to adults sharing his enthusiasm for games. Then Ju-long had told him that most adults feel unsure and clumsy, and they are, because of less training. They may still have the interest, but they put their lives together in such a way that they must prioritise other things.

After lunch, Sarah withdraws with Julia and Augusta, and Peter leaves for some friends. Iona and Jacob clear up after lunch, and Ju-long makes tea and coffee. I set the low table next to the sofa with mugs, milk and Sarah's homemade cookies. I ask for paper and pencil, which makes it easier for me to explain some things I will talk about.

As I sit down in a comfy chair, waiting for the others to show up, I ask Julia to be present and do a melt with me as she did at the council office meeting. She is here before I finish my request. Human thoughts are so slow.

Now, Ju-long and Jacob come with tea and coffee, and Iona comes back after checking up on the girls.

"They are about to take a nap. Later, they will take Julia out in the pushchair. Augusta is very excited, maybe because she is not the youngest in the crowd as she usually is."

I am unsure about what level I should present my story, but Julia sets the tone or vibration, and I follow this like we sing a song together. I start all the way back to when I had watched the movie *The Lord of the Rings* with Cassandra, before I went to Hong Kong, again meeting Ju-long. As I progress, I see our hosts resonate with my story and with the connection to Gaia and reincarnation. Julia tells me that knowledge is "downloaded" in appropriate measures to the couple, now we have introduced them to the resonance of the greater project.

The girls return from their walk, and Augusta comes running into the living room.

"Mum, Dad, I have pushed Julia all by myself and she even didn't cry!" She is warm and takes off her shirt. "Can I have a cookie?"

Jacob gets up. "Let's find some in the kitchen. Take a small basket under the kitchen table for the cookies and I'll find water and some glasses. What about Julia?"

Ju-long answers him. "Sarah has Julia's bottles and she may suck on a whole cookie if Sarah looks after her, but she must not have tiny pieces."

Sarah comes in with Julia, and I hold her for a moment while Augusta and her dad prepare a salver, and Sarah leaves for the bathroom. Jacob carries the salver, while Augusta holds the basket with cookies. I follow them with Julia into Augusta's room.

"This is my room. Here is my bed, and here is the table where I do my homework!"

Jacob smiles. "She wants to do homework like her siblings, so we prepare some tasks for her when she asks for it."

I look around. "What a nice room, Augusta. Some beautiful drawings you have made!"

"I'll draw something for Julia for her room."

"Julia will love that. We'll put it up in a place where she can look at it."

Sarah comes in and takes over Julia, and Jacob and I return to the living room. Now we have a long talk about related things, and it leads to our present situation. I loosely remember the plans for the Dome Home Village, but I'd like an update.

"When can we move into our dome home?"

Jacob only needs a second before he answers. "We count on that all twelve families can move in and celebrate Christmas in their new homes. I have no experience with your electricity generating tiles, but they say that they can finish up in two weeks. We made the latest adjustments to the work plan, and it says you can move in primo October. It is impressive for such a large house. You may still have to work on some other houses to meet your work quota, and the surroundings will still look a total mess. We can't work on the exterior until spring."

Ju-long sums it up for the next stage of work on our house. "Next week we start on the floor and floor heating and prepare the outer surface of the dome for the electricity generating solar tiles. The week after that, they'll start with the tiles themselves."

"I hope Dad will come and look while they are at it, even though he is no expert in this area."

Iona has a comment. "To me, it is not finished before we have completed the exterior. I look forward to the spring, when I can get the garden into shape."

Ju-long is also interested in the garden. "We had a wonderful old garden in Brighton. I have no idea how this one will be. I hope Julia and the local spirits will guide us in that matter."

We leave the Langleys in the afternoon and we are pleased with the outcome of the visit.

It is Tuesday afternoon. This week, Ju-long will work on our house with another man skilled in both wooden floors and floor heating. The outer shell is being prepared for the solar tiles by others after directions from the tile company. They must finish Monday, because some people from the company come Monday morning to start adding the electric-generating solar tiles. Today, I have a paint job in one of the smaller concrete-shell houses with two other women. My phone rings. It is Jacob.

"Hi, Luzi. I've just talked with the council who have just finished a meeting about the road modifications around Dome Home Village. They had good news. There is quite a sum that must be used before the end of the year, or it must be returned to the central administration. To keep the money, the detailed planning must be done and the physical project must be under way before the end of the year. Julia and co. have done a great job!"

"Wow, I'm surprised, even if Julia said it will turn out as it should. It was incredibly fast."

"The chairman told me that they had talked about connecting Fairlight Road and Barley Lane via Til-ekiln Lane, where you live for now, passing the backyard of your new home, but then they have to expropriate pieces of all the lots on both sides of Tilekiln Lane, so they will stick to the plan we've suggested."

"It is fine with us to have the path just outside our perimeters that gives an easy connection for this part of Hastings down to the sea, but a road with cars would not be optimal because we have a lot of kids in the village. Your lot is next to the path as well."

After ending talking with Jacob, Julia pops in with a comment. "Mum, as you can see, things line up perfectly. And this is just the start. Just wait until you can look back a year from now."

"As you have mentioned earlier, I can't even imagine how things will be, dear."

Julia on the nursery and her room

It is 4.10 p.m. and I am on my way home after what feels like a long day painting walls and woodwork. My lower back and up on both sides of my spine hurts. It has been a tedious job, but I have learned things about paint and painting and we have had some nice talks.

This month has been turbulent for all of us, and I think of how a new human like my child must have experienced it. I contact Julia.

"How does baby Julia handle all the new things that happen around her? Especially the different surroundings, new people and all the commotion?"

"You may say that her mind is not bound or polluted by ancestral junk and I, as the I Am, do not attract the negative effects of mass consciousness. Baby Julia, the mind, knows that we are in it together, and that I will always be there to guide her.

She knows that we are one and a trinity at the same time. Her human systems, neurology and the other cells are still not fully matured or ripe, so she is limited in experience of her body as well as the so-called outer world. Emotionally, she feels she is in a protective bubble to a degree, as she did when she was in the womb. She is safe and calm."

"From the other mothers in the birth group, I understand that Julia cries very little compared to the other kids. Or I could say that the other children, as you said, are burdened by ancestral heritage and the influences from mass consciousness."

"Yes, these kids are constantly bombarded with impressions that their system and memories must react to. It is seldom of the pleasant type. You will see that if one of those kids comes into the 'safe bubble' of a harmonious person, they finally relax and are reluctance to leave that person."

"How about when Julia starts in the nursery?"

"I know that both you and Dad have thoughts or worries about this, but I wouldn't allow any misuse of our energies, so it wouldn't happen. Artemis Nursery is a wonderful place, which is being overseen by, well, Artemis, and Sarah will be there at least twelve hours a week as part of her education. It is easy for us to communicate with her."

Julia will start at Artemis Nursery on her sixth month birthday, 6 November, and I will return to more regular work in London. This will, as before, be maybe once or twice a week. Most days, I will work at home. Artemis lies next to our local station, about one and a half miles from our home and about seven minutes by bicycle. It will be easy to deliver Julia there on my way to London by train, or if Ju-long takes the train to Brighton.

As part of training baby Julia to get used to having kids and other adults around, Sarah, Ju-long and I have been visiting The Kids Club, established to take care of the kids when their parents are working at the construction site. We have also arranged two settling sessions at Artemis before she starts there. We had a long talk with Emma, the founder of the Artemis Nursery, to sense into her openness for the situation around Julia. After the meeting, Julia assured us that baby Julia will be fine. We hadn't met Sarah at that point.

Now I am back at our temporary home, where Sarah reads a book and Julia is sleeping. I say hello and take a shower. Ju-long arrives as I come out of the shower. After myself being clean, he stinks of building materials and dust and he takes over the shower.

"Let's have a talk with Sarah when you're finished."

I sit down next to Sarah on the sofa and ask her for a short meeting with me and Ju-long before she leaves for home. She is reading *The Mists of Avalon* by Marion Zimmer Bradley. We talk a little about the book and the different realms that appear in it. I hear Ju-long start the washing machine. I have left my work clothes in there so they can be washed with his. Shortly after, he comes into the living room looking gorgeous. He gives me a quick kiss and sits down on the other side of the table.

"Now you smell much better! How was your day?"

"We have almost finished the floor heating. We will make the rest as we progress with the floors tomorrow. How was your day, dear?"

"After a long day of painting, I need a good back rub to loosen up, but otherwise a good and educational day!"

Ju-long turns to Sarah. "How did your day with our princess go, Sarah?"

"We have been exercising!"

She smiles when she sees his face and explains. "Julia is keen on bringing her nervous system and muscles to optimum conditions. What she really wants is to grow up as fast as possible. She tells me that she both enjoys the experience of being a baby and making that special connection with you, but at the same time she is impatient to grow up, moving ahead with her plans for her human life. Baby Julia has been training coordination, balance and strength. In a gentle way, of course, like we do it at Artemis. For the first time today I saw she can sit up on her own. I could sense her joy in that."

I must smile. "No wonder that she sleeps most of the night."

Sarah laughs. "I can believe that. She tells me that the cells use the calmness of the body to do most of the growth during sleep."

Ju-long asks about their relationship. "How does she communicate with you?"

Julia makes herself known with her scent of wild rose, without letting the others know she has her focus by us.

Sarah explains. "Well, like you, Luzi, have told us. Sometimes it's like a thought, a knowingness, like, this is how it is. Sometimes it feels like it is my intuition, and sometimes she appears as a young adult, either in my environment, or she invites me to some place like Elvendale. At one time, she took me to visit the Sun, and we were right inside it without feeling the slightest bit warm. It was just like being here in the living room. I connected to the Sun's consciousness, and it was such a wonderful and touching experience."

I want to know how she can use this at Artemis. "How open can you be about this way of communication at the nursery?"

"I've talked with Julia about this. For now, I feel I can talk about spirits of nature and I'm known to be quite intuitive. When Julia stays there regularly, the consciousness will allow people to resonate with a higher truth and be more trustful of their own intuition. As we open the area for more acceptance, children of high awareness will come to Artemis, and so will new staff members. I look forward to this expansion."

Julia whispers to me with a smile. "As you know, it will reach much further than Artemis. It still depends on people being ready for the opening or nothing will change."

I would ask her about London, but she gives the answer before I can put my question into words. "It doesn't take more candles to bring light to many people in a room than if there were but a few."

I smile an inner smile. "You sound like me, when I speak as my master self!"

I am sure Sarah would like to go home, so I change the subject in the external conversation. "Sarah, what date will you start college?"

"October 8. It's a Tuesday. About that. I might have a 'stand-in' for me as a babysitter for Julia if you're interested."

"Oh, we are, but I hope you may still come by now and then when you can schedule your time. Who is it you recommend?"

"Her name is Cloe. She works part time at Artemis and holds an Early Age Teacher status. She is twenty-seven years old, a single mum with a six-year-old boy. Cloe has her parents living close by, and the boy spends time with them. I think she has a degree in sales or office work too."

"Could you bring Cloe to meet us? An evening maybe?"

"I will contact her this evening and get back to you. You will be at the construction site next week, so she might come before I leave after babysitting Julia."

"That'll be fine. Yes, I'll spend some days painting the interior in our own house. After that, I will be back in 'construction'. I like to shift between the different kinds of work to keep the variation."

Ju-long clears up a few things about our schedule. "I'll be at the university in Brighton all weekdays and I won't be working late. As you know, we'll be home on the weekend, so we all have the weekend off!"

Sarah leaves and shortly after I breastfeed Julia while Ju-long starts on the dinner. When Julia has eaten, we switch so Ju-long makes her ready for bed and I take over the dinner.

Anna calls us in the evening. She is in her apartment in London. We talk a little about her life in London and her studies, and then she wants to know about the dome house.

"What about Julia's room? We have been working a lot to make her comfortable with the room in Brighton and now she gets a new room here."

"We have been here about a month, so I don't think it matters much. We'll use the same colours on the walls, the floor will be wood as well, and she will have her things. Julia tells us not to worry. I'll be painting the walls next week. The outer walls are both walls and the roof, so I have to find out if I should use two different colours or just one colour."

Julia laughs. "It'll be much more artistic than that."

She shows me an inner image of how she wants it to be. The room has only one wall connected to the outside and it curves up and becomes the ceiling, the other walls are vertical. The colour will gradually change from white at the bottom to sky blue where it meets the back wall. The wall opposite the curved one has the door and will have trees and be a forest, and the walls at each side will be a lush meadow leading up to the trees.

I am very sceptical.

"I can't do that!"

Julia sends a calming smile.

"We WILL do that. In no-time it's already done, and it looks beautiful and will be shamelessly admired!"

Anna laughs on the phone.

"Julia shows me the room. Pretty cool, sis!"

"I thought I was just going to use the painting roller, but this seem to be quite a project on its own."

Anna wants to know when we will be ready to move in. "When can I expect to help you move in?"

"We expect it to be three to four weeks from now. I look forward to it. I'm tired of living in someone else's house and doing all this work on the site. Well, I learn things, skills, and I get to know my neighbours in a way I probably wouldn't have done otherwise, but I guess I have grown impatient to live there."

It is always a joy to talk to Anna, and I wish she lived closer to us. And my parents too.

Family visits

The clock shows 4.04 when I wake up. It is Monday and I start painting our home today. I have decided to paint Julia's room last. It gives me time to consider my strategy.

Today I will work with Joyce who has many years of experience with painting and decoration. I talk to her about Julia's room and she comes up with some great ideas. The white-to-blue toning will be made by starting with the blue paint and then gradually add more and more white to it. For the other things, she suggests that I look at some rollers with textures. I am excited and drive to Winchester's Building Supplies in Old London Road in the afternoon. I have the white paint, but need blue, green and brown.

"Can I help you?"

I turn around and Julia stands right in front of me with a big smile, looking as pretty as ever. She wears a small blue top, white shorts and gold sandals.

"Remember, I said that WE will do this thing together. You have the note with the data for the white paint. We just need to pick a blue, a red and a yellow bucket and then mix the colours to green and brown ourselves. We must have twice as much blue as yellow and half as much red as yellow. Let's go looking at the rollers first. We need some sponges to dab on paint as well."

We find a roller with a texture that makes a bark pattern for the tree trunks and branches. I end up picking a ragged roller to use for the leaves, and one for tall grass and some flower stampers.

"We'll use different tones to get more variation. Don't worry, Mum, this will be great!"

It is strange to walk here with my grown-up daughter, picking tools to paint the room for the baby of the same girl. Now I can't wait to get started. As I approach the counter to get the basic blue, yellow and red paint mixed to the colours Julia and I had agreed upon, I sense a hug and a touch on my cheek as a goodbye.

Ju-long is home when I arrive. He is in the kitchen preparing dinner while baby Julia sits in the lying chair next to him, holding a carrot with both hands. It is so large that she can't bite off pieces and choke on them. I kiss them both before I take a quick shower. I know baby Julia is hungry and wants her milk. When I come back to the kitchen, I tell Ju-long about my shopping adventure with Julia.

Ju-long comments with a smile. "This parentship is so out of the ordinary or, better said, so much more. At some point, we'll only have one."

"I'm grateful that Julia chose to have a near-normal

childbirth and give us the opportunity to experience her growing up."

After breastfeeding Julia and on my way to the bathroom to bathe her, Dad calls. "Hi everyone. I just want to say goodnight to the princess. Oh, there she is!"

We use the camera on the phone. Julia can see the motion of Dad's face, but I think it is his voice that attracts her most. She makes "talking" sounds and smiles, knowing it always pays back with a response from Granddad. He tells us that Mum and he will show up sometime Friday before noon, and he will check up on the house and the work with the solar tiles. Because so much has happened since I last saw my parents, it feels as if it has been ages, even though it has only been five weeks. We say goodbye to Dad; Mum is not there for the moment. And then I make Julia ready for bed.

Now I want to finish the painting on Thursday afternoon, so I call Jacob to ask if he can assign one or two more, besides Joyce and me.

"Tomorrow may be a little too soon, but I might find one for Wednesday and Thursday."

"That would be so great. Thanks, Jacob, and say hello to your family!"

Tuesday it turns out to be more difficult to raise the work force and I get a little frustrated. Julia brings me back to calmness.

"Relax, Mum. My room doesn't even need to be finished on Thursday or Friday. Why don't you ask Grandma to bring some working cloths and you can do it together when she comes Friday?"

"That would be so great! Mum and I have done nothing like that for … well, I don't remember. Only the rooms which demand installations, like the kitchen, bathroom and laundry, need to be finished."

Of course, Mum wants to help, especially with Julia's room. She is an artist, after all. It works out better than I could have expected.

I don't want to paint the doors of the built-in cabinets in Julia's room. They have a wooden structure, but are too large, lack strong, coloured grains and will stand out. I call Mum and ask Mum what to do.

"Get a curtain or a tablecloth with a suitable motif and we'll find a way to attach it to the doors."

I ended up finding a shower curtain with birch trees, wide enough to cover both doors. I just have to cut it in two. More so, Thursday evening all rooms were painted, including walls and woodwork, except Julia's room. It proves all my worries to be the work of my old mind.

Julia jokes with me. "You should ask your mind to mind its own business!"

"Eh, and what is that?"

"Enjoy life and be happy. This is ultimately what the mind wants. You're here to take care of the rest, the I Am and the Master Wisdom."

"And the brain?"

"The brain will take care of the bodily functions, including receiving instructions from you."

It is Friday morning and I have a question for Julia. "If I tell baby Julia that her grandparents are coming today, will she then understand it?"

"Her awareness is mostly outside of space-time even though she understands time. What will happen is that she connects her memories and her awareness with them and knows when they will arrive. In a way, she has already experienced their visit and followed their thoughts and feelings about the visit on their way home. She knows the events that are most likely to happen."

My parents have started out early from Sevenoaks and arrive just before 9 a.m. Dad's copper metallic Tesla S finds its way to the narrow Tilekiln Lane and parks next to our car. Ju-long has left for the university in Brighton. I have arranged with Sarah that she come at 10 a.m. and not 7.45 a.m. as she would normally do when I must work at the construction site. It will be the first time Sarah meets my parents.

The next hour we spend enjoying each other's company, my parents having much attention for their first grandchild. Sarah comes at five to ten and, after a little talk, Mum, Dad and I walk to the construction site. It is about one hundred yards. Jacob has arranged that someone install the kitchen and bathrooms today, rather than next week. Next week they will install the heat pumps and other technical installations.

Mum has not been to the site before, but we have shown her pictures of the house, both inside and outside. She looks a little around until Dad points at the house.

"It's this one!"

"Oh man, it's much larger than I expected. Is there only one floor?"

Dad explains. "Yes, dear. As you can see, the shape is not quite a half sphere. The walls start more vertical and the top ends more horizontal. The more vertical walls are practical to give more space, and by curving the roof into being more horizontal, less heat will go to waste. You still have a nice tall ceiling."

When we arrive, Dad shouts to the men working on the outside of the dome with the tiles that he will be with them shortly and then follows us inside. There are a lot of large boxes in different sizes in the living room. This is the stuff for the kitchen, bathroom and cabinets. We say hello to people working here while we make a quick tour.

Dad nods. "I'm impressed about the quality of the work. I have arranged to meet Jacob Langley in the

196

afternoon, but right now I'll talk with the tile work-ers. Enjoy your artwork, girls!"

Mum and I enter what will become Julia's room.

"Well, let's make a plan, Luzi! I guess your friend is right about starting with the blue and gradually mixing in the white. Then we must start with the scaffold to get close enough to the ceiling to see what we're doing."

"So, first the sky, down to the window and glass door to the outside. Next the back wall with the door and the forest, still with the scaffold in the same place. It is a wooden door, so it's fine and doesn't need any paint."

I am glad to have Mum doing this with me, and we both sense Julia being present in the work. We quickly get the hang of it. We must add a little wa-ter to make the paint merge better or it will dry too fast when added to the wall.

Dad comes at exactly noon to pick us up for lunch. He knocks at the closed door. It goes inwards so we have to keep it closed while we work on the wall around it.

"What a beautiful sky; just like looking out of the opening in an observatory at daytime. He turns around. "I am right on time. You've just finished the background for the forest."

We both get a kiss and Mum looks at our progress.

"It went well, but we won't finish it all today. When

you get the hang of the trees and leaves, you will finish it on the weekend."

We walk back to Sarah and Julia and prepare a wonderful lunch out of things Mum and Dad have brought. Dad could just invite us all to dinner somewhere in Hastings, but we have a tradition of making and sharing our meals. This way we are more appreciative of the food and we, to a high degree, know what is in it. I realise that having Sarah around will very much be like having Julia in the family later, when she grows up.

While Dad prepares some smoked trout fillets, he tells us a little about his first impressions.

"I have been around the whole site and am impressed. Most of the houses have been closed, meaning that the they have windows and doors. Some need the outside shielded, usually the concrete ones, while the rest need the inner walls or inner shell with insulation. The overall planning seems to work so the houses will be finished at approximately the same time. Christmas, will be my guess. I am sure that other projects will benefit from your experiences. I can see that there is some heavy machinery at Barley Lane, so I expect that they will start up Monday or at least next week."

This is new to me. "I haven't noticed the machines. I always come in from the other side. Well, unless we cross Barley Lane to go to the small lake or down to the beach."

Dad refers to the work with the tiles. "About your house. The tile people will bring the control units and batteries on Monday and install it in the laundry room. They expect to be finished Wednesday evening."

After lunch I use the chance to breastfeed Julia, before passing her over to Sarah. I am glad that we have Sarah, who seems to be such a good match to Julia.

Dad is not in a hurry. "I'll rest in the garden, because there is still over an hour till my meeting with Mr Langley."

"Yes, do that, Carl. In the meantime, Luzi and I will create a forest and a meadow."

"See you, Dad. I expect Ju-long to be home about 4 p.m."

The house is empty when Mum and I arrive. No one except maybe me will work here on the weekend. I want to finish all the painting so the smell can leave the house before we move in. I know they have been working in the two bathrooms this morning, so we make a quick check. They are both finished with everything, even the lamps and the hooks for the towels.

Ju-long has told me that the cabinets and other stuff in the laundry room will be installed at the same time as the tile workers, install their technical equipment, because it will be stored in one of the cabinets. The cabinets, sinks, washing machine and dryer are in their boxes in the living room. Only the water heater and the heat pumps are connected and placed in a special cabinet, secured to the wall.

A computer will run programs for ventilation, room and water heating and the electrical system that feeds electricity to the house from the tiles. The house will run on its other power for quite some time in case of a power failure in the electricity coming from the power grid.

Mum and I build up the forest, which background is dry enough for us to add trunks, branches and leaves to. The underlying leaves are the darkest. Then we add a little yellow and some white to the dark green, as we did with the sky, so we end up with light green leaves like a beech forest in spring. I will work on the undergrowth later.

We take a break and Mum looks at the shower curtain with the birches. The built-in cabinet with two sliding doors is close to the glass door to the outside and on the "meadow". The birches will be in the foreground of that part of the meadow.

"Here is what I think. The two sliding doors are overlapping a bit even when they are closed. The curtain is more than wide enough, so you might find a suitable spot to cut it in two pieces. There is only a narrow gap when the doors slide beside each other. Because of the folds, you need to iron the parts, but with a low temperature, because it's made of plastic and not meant to be ironed. Get some Velcro and add it to the edges of the doors and to the curtains. You will need someone to help you with that."

With that solved, we move on with the forest and continue it on the two walls with the meadow, with ever smaller trees so the forest appears to follow the meadow into the distant.

At some point I hear Dad talking outside and, soon after, he shows up in company with Jacob. "My girls have been busy, I see."

Mum stretches her back. "Yes, we have about an hour and then we can stop for today, clean up and come over for afternoon tea."

Dad turns to me. "I have been talking with Jacob and have some good news that may stress you if you choose."

"Well, just come out with it, Dad."

"The tile people will finish Wednesday next week, and the kitchen and the laundry room as well sometime in the same week. Surely the heat pump control and the other programs must be up and running as well. So why not move in next weekend?"

"What? But, well, yeah. It's two weeks earlier than we have expected!"

Dad smiles. "I think you should plan to move in next Friday, dear. Mum and I will come and give a hand. You should invite Anna as well!"

Jacob is joyful as well. "So, my 'early in October' becomes 'at the end of September' instead. That's great! It will also free up some working people to help finishing other houses. Let's talk, say Wednesday, when we should move the container with all your stuff close to the front door."

Dad prepares to leave. "I'll go and prepare the afternoon tea and then we'll see each other in about an hour."

Jacob leaves as well. "Say hello to the princess from me!"

Later, as we clean up our tools, Mum asks me if we have a playpen. "Now that Julia can sit up on her own, it won't be long before she moves around. As you don't use carpets, she might find a way to glide on the floor like a penguin."

This creates an inner picture of Julia in a penguin costume speeding around in the house.

"We have talked about that, even in the beginning. We feel she should not be penned in. It is up to us to create a safe environment, so she has the whole house to explore. There is no second floor, nor a cellar. We will usually keep the door to the laundry room and technical equipment closed. The most critical cabinet doors in there will need a special tool to open them, and the rest have child-safe blockers on them."

Ju-long is back from work when we arrive for tea. Sarah, who has no grandparents left, says yes when Mum invites her to stay for tea. I wish Anna was here too.

Sarah leaves after having tea, and Mum and Dad drive back to Sevenoaks after dinner. We will see them next weekend when they come and help us move into our new dome home.

This evening I call Anna and we have a long talk. She has preparations to do for some upcoming exams at the university in London, and her friend Jo-Ann will visit her family in Denmark. Anna comes up with the brilliant idea that she can take over the caretaker role at the house on Tilekiln Lane as we move into our new house. She wants to share the babysitter role with Cloe when Sarah starts at college in a little over two weeks.

After the talk with Anna, I write an e-mail to Mr and Ms Brandon about Anna's suggestion of taking care of their house until December when she must be back in London.

They reply that they have added Anna to the contract and make a remark about a reduced rent, which is already low, if only Anna is living in the house.

On the weekend I finish Julia's room. When we visit the house with Julia, Sunday, Ju-long helps me with the Velcro and the shower curtains so the birches stand beautifully on the meadow. We have chosen not to have any wall cupboards in the kitchen. There are only different kinds of drawers, even in the sockets below the actual drawers. This way the kitchen looks more open.

This is the week when we will move into our lovely new home. Monday is 23 September, and the autumn has started with much rain. I hope it will take a break on the weekend. Working people are busy in the house, and in the afternoon I can see that the kitchen takes form.

The tile people finish late Wednesday, so they will use Thursday to test the system when there is light on the tiles. Everything else is ready for us to move in. I have arranged with Jacob that our container is placed at the front door, and a large steel plate will cover the wet soil that hasn't been covered with slabs yet. We will probably use the entrance at the laundry room this winter because the floor here is easy to clean up after dirty boots.

Anna comes with our parents Friday morning. She has taken the train the day before from London to Sevenoaks, which is just south of the capital.

We start with a late breakfast before we go to the container. The whole UK family is in the dome house. Ju-long and I have been introduced to the programs that control different aspects of the house and are confident about moving in. The ventilation is running on high speed to remove the smell of the building materials, including the painting and the cabinets.

Late in the afternoon the container is empty, and most of our things are piled up in the living room. Mum and Dad decide to stay overnight. They choose Northrise Lodge, which is only two hundred yards from where Anna will sleep, as she will stay in the house on Tilekiln Lane. We will arrange breakfast in the morning. Anna persuades us to get dinner from New Hong Kong Kitchen, which didn't take much effort.

Saturday, most of our things are placed in cabinets

or drawers, and the empty, collapsed cardboard boxes are in the container. Others can use them when they move their things to their new dome homes. The container will be picked up on Monday. The living room looks a little empty, but rather that than stuffed. Mum and Dad leave in the afternoon. They have been a great help and they are always nice to have around. Dad has arranged a small car for Anna so she can move around more freely. She doesn't feel she will have much use for it, but I bet that when she has experienced the freedom the car gives her, she will not part with it.

New home and new community

It is the last day of the first week in our new home. Sunday 6 October, on Julia's five months birthday, she celebrates it with showing us she can wriggle towards a toy. We are all excited, including Julia. I believe Mum is right when she told me that it won't be long before she moves around.

Ju-long and I are still working on the construction site to help to finish other houses so all have time to settle in well before Christmas. We are halfway through the twelve homes. Jacob and the others in management of the site have put 1 December to be the finishing day, which is also the first Sunday of Advent.

My sister, Anna, and our new babysitter, Cloe, are taking turns with Sarah taking care of Julia. Anna needs some time away from her studies and I like having her around.

Through the people in this area I get more knowledge of the area we now live in. Ore is the name of the village that is now a part of Hastings. The Ore Local Private Committee is active in promoting the Dome Home Village, which is on the outskirts of the former village, to bring more life to the area. The committee is a frequent user of the Ore Community Centre at Old London Road.

It was sad to hear that the local library in Ore is permanently closed, and people are referred to eLibrary. Luckily, the free Home Library Service is available for disabled, frail or persons who are caring for someone who cannot be left, and is run by volunteers.

Hasting Library at the Town Centre, on the other hand, is impressive, with a beautifully restored building. It has a great selection of books in the children's section. The library has many comput-ers that give people the opportunity for study or courses. On the second floor there is a learning cen-tre, and the staff is friendly and helpful.

On 8 October, on her birthday, babysitter Sarah starts at college here in Hastings studying *early years*. It seems that Julia, Anna and Cloe are getting along well. Anna has her studies and Cloe her oth-er jobs, but they make it work fine.

Do you mind?

Now we have been in our new house for a month. I come home from a working trip to London and find Ju-long and Julia sitting on the large mat next to the door to the main entrance.

"Hello, my loved ones, what are you doing down there?"

"Julia asked me to place baby Julia on the mat. She wanted to show me that she can crawl. And she does!"

208

"Oh, the floor is too smooth and her legs are slipping if she has her rompers on!"

"Yes, maybe we should buy her a rug after all."

I can see Ju-long smiles, so I know that he hears Julia as well as I do.

"Don't bother. Soon I'll be up and running. Just let me have bare knees. The floor is warm, clean and all right."

I will mention that baby Julia is now five and a half months old.

Earlier today, Anna texted me and asked if she could visit us later today, so I invited her to dinner.

After dinner, with Julia tucked in and Ju-long working in the study, Anna and I sit on the sofa with our tea mugs. I wait for Anna to start. She holds her mug with both hands as if she is cold and draws warmth from it.

"For two days I have not been well, and this report I am writing as part of my studies is killing me! I'm tense in the neck muscles and under the shoulder blades and I get terrible headaches. When I get up in the morning, I feel worse than when I went to bed."

I sense my Master Wisdom and my I Am flanking the human part; not with inner pictures, but as a knowingness of the trinity. Most of the time we are just trinity without me being aware of it, but as I open to my sister, I notice the trinity, not like being a part of the trinity, but me being the trinity.

"As I have experienced during the last couple of years, my mind, which I see as both the mental and the emotional part, is easily overloaded. It was my non-human parts that wanted to get my attention on the mind taking tasks it either couldn't nor shouldn't solve. It became my job to convince the mind to let go of these tasks it was never meant to complete and hand them to the Master Wisdom and the I Am."

"I remember you have talked about this before."

"I have, and now I'm convinced that your mind will listen to what I have to say. I ask your mind not to take a defensive position, because I'll grant it great wisdom and start by talking in general terms."

Anna smiles. "Now your vocabulary changes to be somehow old fashioned, as it sometimes does."

I can hear it myself and smile. I enjoy feeling so complete, as I do when the trinity steps forward in this way. If I was talking to a person who does not know me well, I would be more careful with what words and phrases I would use; here I can just let it flow.

"Indeed, we are of many eras and we draw from many voices. Let's begin. First, we must distinguish the brain and the mind. The brain is the physical apparatus, including the chemical and the electromagnetic system. The mind is the psycho-emotional awareness. The human mind is an imitator. The body can run mostly autonomous of

210

the brain and has its own communication system. The tasks the brain must do, according to the body, will in no way get it out of idle mode. The mind is a control freak that has taken over the control FROM the body and that has greatly increased its work load. The mind has also imitated the senses of the I Am and created your commonly known senses, like sight and hearing. This has dulled the original senses of the body. The feelings of the I Am have been imitated to become the human's emotions. The mind has also imitated the Master Wisdom by overusing its memory capacity and its mental calculating capacity. From mostly running idle, the mind is now running full speed all the time. Even when the body sleeps."

"Wow, now I feel even worse! I can see where the headaches come from, but what about the pain in the neck and under the shoulder blades?"

"As we told you, the mind is heavily invested in the control of the body. The overload extends into the rest of the body, causing many illnesses, including cancer or complete mental breakdown as the most extreme. That is why stress is so invalidating."

"So, my mind must stop being such a control freak!"

"To lose control feels very frightening and fear is a basic human emotion; very difficult to work with. The mind will feel it loses itself, as in going out of your mind, and, in a way, dies. The fear will be the fear of dying!"

Anna looks puzzled and in despair. "How can we

even talk to the mind about letting go if it goes into fear mode?"

"We can't have a dialogue with the emotional part of the mind. It wouldn't listen to reason. We must talk to its logics, so here we go."

Anna nods and I sense the energies are shifting when I proceed. I start with a punch to the soft belly of the logical mind. "You know that the mind can't do the job; can't create your life. If it could, your life would look differently I bet!"

Now I speak to the whole human part of Anna. "The fear of letting go is from our human part, as you know. It is natural and we must accept that. We must treat the human part as a child, because it is a child; maybe with many years of life experience, but still a child. It is all about allowing and acceptance, but it will take a lot of trusting for the human part. It must trust YOU, the I Am and the Master Wisdom, and realise the trinity!"

Now I pull out the carrot, the reward. "Imagine, when the mind calms down and the I AM and the Master Wisdom run the show, how easy it will be for the trinity, which includes the mind. BUT the mind must have experienced A LOT where it sees the I Am and the Master Wisdom are successful and life runs smooth to give over the 'job'. The fear will come back again and again until the mind finally allows and enjoys the life in trinity."

Anna smiles. "So, do you live without a mind?"

"Oh, if I don't mind!"

We both laugh, and the energies loosen again after so much talk of fear.

I continue in the lighter energy. "The mind is part of the human and part of the experience of being a human. The mind also has a memory and deep emotional traces that certain events might trigger. If that wasn't the case, you wouldn't be human but a robot, and who wants to live like a robot, easy life or not?"

"I bet some will."

"You're right; a lot of people will!"

"Are you not using your mind while you're writing? You do a lot of writing."

"I use the mind, but not that much. As soon as it goes out of idle mode, I get restless and need to get up and walk around a bit. I feel much like a cat that all of a sudden changes activity or starts grooming. The same happens if I feel tired during work. Then I can get up and walk towards the couch to lie down for a few minutes, but, before reaching the couch, I'm ready to continue my work."

Anna speaks her mind. "I think we all get those signals, but we just don't pay attention. Instead, we focus even more on the task we are doing."

"I think that's true. We blame ourselves for not concentrating and then push our mind both emotionally and mentally even further."

The simplicity of allowing

"And the method is allowing?"

"Allowing is not a method. How can it be a method? You simply allow yourself, meaning the trinity, and that's that. FULL STOP."

"But the mind?"

"Treat it like the child it is. SHOW it the life with the trinity. Only by experiencing will it build up the evidence to trust in letting go."

"The mind can't really allow, right? It experiences me allowing and it experiences the success of the I Am and the Master Wisdom in action."

"Exactly! The trust will build up, but sometimes fear will be triggered and you must hold its hand and guide it through the fearful experience."

"But if I am the one who is doing the allowing of the I Am and the Master Wisdom, who am I?"

I send a smile with a wink to my sister. "Only a mind would ask such a question!"

"No, seriously?"

"Maybe there is a human part outside the mind."

"You're playing tricks with me, sis!"

"Your Master Wisdom has experienced all human lives, so ..."

Anna lights up and smiles. "Ah, we're tricking the one, you know who!"

I loosen up some of Anna's muscles in the neck and shoulders and then she leaves after saying good night to Ju-long, promising to do no mental stuff at all and go to bed.

Shortly after, Ju-long comes out from the study and we enjoy the evening together.

The Kitten and the Lion

Today it is 6 November, and Julia's six-month birthday and the day she starts in Artemis Nursery. Ju-long brings her there and Sarah is there as part of the education, so we know our daughter will be in good hands. I am working at home today, and even I know that Julia will be fine. I have checked my phone is fully charged and the ring tone is on. I am still a human parent sending her offspring away for the first time. After delivering Julia, Ju-long takes the train to Brighton.

Sarah calls at noon telling me that everything has been fine and she has observed that Julia had pulled herself up into a standing position. She really wants to be an active player at the nursery. Cloe will take over and look after her in the afternoon.

After Sarah's call I am restless, looking forward to picking up Julia. I arrive at 3 p.m. sharp and Cloe tells me that Julia has had a nice afternoon. She has not been crying but has been alert of what had been going on around her and has been baby talking a lot. I guess it was like when we were visiting The Kids Club established for the construction site. I text Ju-long the good news, and he can call me when he has the time.

Julia jumps in with a comment. "Don't worry, be happy; because I am!"

When we are home, I give Julia a bath. She acts overexcited as if the many impressions of the day have charged her to max. After having her milk, she looks tired, and I lay her in bed. Later, Ju-long calls and is excited about Julia's first day at Artemis. He gives me an estimate of when he will be home.

Ju-long arrives about 5.30 p.m. and Julia wakes up. He wants to see for himself that Julia can pull herself up. When she does it, I realise that it is the strength of her legs that is doing most of the job and she uses her hands to keep the balance and not fall over. From now on, it will be actual walking "exercises" that is in focus to improve the coordination of her leg movements and balance of the body.

Ju-long and I have agreed that Julia should sleep in her own room when she is six months old. I guess her body and mind will be so exhausted this evening she will sleep most of the night. There is a bathroom between her room and ours, but we will keep the doors open. We don't use a baby monitor.

Tomorrow I will drive her to Artemis, and Ju-long will pick her up when he returns from Brighton.

The first night Julia spent in her own room did not differ from any other night. I had been thinking what would happen if she woke up and couldn't hear anyone breathing in the room. She wakes up around 6 a.m. and uses her attention call as she always does. Ju-long and I get up and start our day.

The week after she can get up on her own, Julia

walks around by holding on to things. She still crawls, but it is clear that there is some training going on, urged by the mature part of her. We are playing and stimulate her in many ways, but we also have what we call being-time, where we are together doing nothing other than being aware of each other.

There is less and less work to do on the remaining homes, and Ju-long is not on the schedule anymore. During the winter, there will be some planning meetings for the spring.

Anna has moved back to London to finish the project she has been working on for almost two months. Ju-long and I must keep an eye on the Brandon's house until they return from New Zealand in primo January.

In the third week of November, all dome homes are finished and all families have moved in. Ju-long and I walk with Julia in the pushchair in the early evening and see Christmas decorations and lights signalling this special time of the year.

It is Sunday 1 December and Julia surprises us by walking from the living room to the kitchen without holding on to anything. This is the first time we have observed her doing that. She was playing at the low table with some of her toys. She has a soft toy cat in her hand and she toddles to Ju-long and I who are preparing dinner in the kitchen section. It is an open environment so we can keep an eye on her while she is playing. She shows me the cat, and

I get a picture of the cat she and I saw this summer by a pile of stones on a field with cattle. The lion goddess Sekhmet visited us in the guise of a large orange cat with fluffy fur.

"Oh, you want a real cat in the family, love!"

I refresh Ju-long on the incident I told him about months ago.

Ju-long is a bit sceptical.

"Is she really able to remember this?"

Julia answers him.

"Oh Dad, baby Julia took in the encounter with all her senses. A fluffy cat's tail, gently striking her face, will connect with the pure joy of being met with great compassion by the consciousness you know as Sekhmet. I urged her to bring the toy cat to you."

I will try, as I have come to adore the cats I have encountered lately.

"We could search for a long-haired and orange Maine Coon, but what age and sex?"

"A kitten we'll have longer and a female would not have to defend her space to the same degree as a male."

"It is quite early for our daughter to start making such kind of demands, love!"

"Dear Luzi, I am pretty sure that her requests in the coming years will be reasonable and with arguments we can't top."

I lift up Julia and the cat and walk back to the living room.

"We'll find a nice cat for the family, love. It might take a little while."

"You should know better, Mum! Why would I bring up the cat if it was not the time?"

"You brought up your brother, and THAT was not the right time!"

"Well, that was the right time to bring it up AND it was so thrilling to sense you being totally surprised."

Baby Julia and I play a little with the cat and I do the tail thing with her face, which she loves, and she shrieks in ecstasy. Then it seems the right time for her breastfeed. We have got a high chair made of bamboo so after the milk she sits with us at the table, trying out some foods as well while we have dinner.

After dinner, Ju-long makes Julia ready and tucks her in, while I clean up after dinner. When I hear it is the time, I walk in, giving Julia a goodnight kiss. There is no problem with Julia sleeping in her own room. Julia has explained this.

"Baby Julia does not need another person to feel safe and her room feels as comfy as anywhere. She does not know the feeling of being abandoned and lonely, and she knows that she will ALWAYS get the assistance she requires. She is the master in her own life. She is the trinity and doesn't feel separate from it."

"But if we see the mind of baby Julia as the human, she must realise that the I Am and the Master is something else."

"She has known nothing else, so to her 'this is me'. It differs greatly from how an ordinary person will perceive itself."

Ju-long comes back from Julia's room and sits next to me on the sofa. "It still fascinates me that when I look into her eyes, I look right into her soul. I've done it thousands of times, but it's still a great wonder."

I give him a hug. "And now we will become cat parents as well, love. Take the computer and let's make a search. I'm sure someone will watch over our shoulders."

After twenty minutes I become impatient. Julia had been talking about the right time or something like that, but nothing of interest has come up.

Julia comments on my impatience. "Instead of broadening your search you could broaden your perspective. There is a difference. Maybe the cat is not in a stray cat home. Maybe she is not even for sale. Or maybe she is NOT to be found on the Internet?"

I think I heard the capital NOT.

"How can we find anything if it's not on the Internet?"

Julia sighs. "There is actually a life outside the Internet. Just listen to some of your neighbours on the cat subject."

Ju-long lightens up. "Neighbours!"

Ju-long calls Jacob and I can sense his answer being a question: A cat? Dear Ju-long had failed to bring some background to his question so Jacob tries to make sense of it. Ju-long gets it and tells about Julia's request.

Ju-long's phone is now on speaker and I hear Jacob laugh. "Six months old and she makes requests. The next thing will be an elephant and you must buy the whole area down to the Channel!"

I raise my voice to ensure Jacob hears me. "Hi, Jacob. For now, it's just a long-haired Maine Coon cat. We'll deal with the elephant if it comes up. We can always send Julia with a travelling circus."

"Hi, Luzi. Oh, I so love that girl! The village has an online board and there is a physical one at Simonson in number 95. You can post a request there yourself."

I remember the online board. "I've seen the online board and even read it now and then, but I don't get to the official entrance often unless I use the car."

Ju-long ends the talk with Jacob. "We'll post on both boards. Thanks, Jacob."

"Say hello to your family, Jacob!"

"Thanks, Luzi, I will. Remember to advertise for some cat stuff and some grooming gear for the long fur."

Now we make two identical posts with different headlines, one about the kitten and the other about the cat gear. Ju-long puts up the printed post at the board at the village's entrance. He comes back and reports that there were no posts of cats at all, and we post both on the village web page as well. Now we browse the Internet to find out more about the Maine Coon.

I find a photo of a cute kitten. "I wonder what name we should give such a cute little thing, Ju-long."

The name comes promptly to both of us—BOOM-ER—before he can think of an answer.

Julia explains. "This is the name baby Julia chose."

I associate the name with a character in *Battlestar Galactica*, which is my favourite space series: lieutenant Sharon "Boomer" Valerii, brought forth by Grace Park. Still, I can't get any association between the cat and the name.

"Don't look for a meaning of the word; feel the punch you get in your solar plexus when you imagine the SOUND."

"I can imagine the low frequency punch, but I wouldn't say that fluffy tail fur in the face would make me feel BOOM, even if it was the first experience of that kind in my life."

"Then think of suddenly 'standing' heart to heart with the lion goddess, Sekhmet, and her immense 'strength'."

"That gives more sense, indeed! They have met before the tail thing."

Julia continues, "You don't have to know everything about the breed. Every creature is unique and this one will be as special as dealing with the whole of me, the one you know as Julia. Get the basics and the rest will come."

I make a folder called Boomer on my computer and add it to The Cloud too. Here we put links and other stuff about our little new family member we haven't even seen yet.

It is time for bed. While brushing my teeth, I think of another little male member who might announce his arrival within a year or so. I already feel a connection of love, and now that I open to it, tears roll down my cheeks. It is even stronger than I remember the first connection with Julia. Ju-long sees my tears, but I signal "OK" with a thumb up before I rinse my mouth.

"I'll tell you in bed, dear!"

He is used to my tears, and I see him checking up on Julia before going to the bedroom.

The next day, Monday 2 December, the post is set up at the Ore Community Centre and the local shopping centre. The same evening, it is the Ore Community Centre post that gives the hit about the kitten. It is not a professional breeder, but the cats are Mrs Fleet's passion. Amanda and her husband, Kevin, are managers of the Spindlewook Country Holiday Park situated one mile to the north-west of our home. They seem to be kind people and, at the same time, interested in our village and its "energy" and have followed it from the very start. Amanda has a three-month-old kitten. She is not sterilised and was not meant for sale, but maybe breeding if she turned out right. We plan to visit them the next day in the late afternoon. Ju-long can't be back from work earlier. It suits them fine. The caravan season has just ended and they are making the last preparations to close the park for the winter this week.

Tuesday I am working at home, but Ju-long has some work to do in London. Ju-long's phone rings at 6.16 a.m. It is about his appointment in London. He briefs me after the talk.

"It was the manager of the book restoration of the British Library in Euston Road. He has been sick most of the night and cannot instruct me in the job we have planned. I now have a whole day without plans."

"You know, I'll be working at home, so let us pick

Julia up after her lunch nap. You can take the car and deliver her to Artemis this morning and tell them we will pick her up early. I'll call Amanda and ask her if we can come earlier."

It is OK if we come earlier; Amanda is home all day. If she is not in the house answering the door, we can just call.

In the early afternoon, we pick up Julia and get the chance to say hello to Sarah. She laughs when she hears about the cat. On Julia's request we have the pushchair in the back of the car. "I want to be close to the ground when meeting Boomer."

Soon we are at the holiday park and Amanda comes out of the reception to greet us when we leave the parking lot. She must have seen us through the window which has a sign saying CLOSED.

Ju-long pushes Julia. She shows us through the reception and out the back and over a courtyard to their own house. I have only told her that we have a daughter who is six months, but now I tell her about Julia coming with her toy cat, walking independently for the first time, and about her meeting with the orange Maine Coon in Brighton. We sit down in a large kitchen where an adult orange Maine Coon sleeps on a chair, raising its head as we come in.

"It is the mother, Stella. Where is the little one?"

She looks around, but then the cutest bundle of

orange fur comes into the kitchen from inside the house to see what is going on.

"Here she is. If we have kittens in the winter, they are in the kitchen with their mother. She has two brothers, but they may make trouble somewhere else in the house. Is tea fine with you?"

Ju-long and I agree.

She looks down at the kitten. "What do you think of these nice people?"

The kitten doesn't seem shy and is probably used to many people around her. She starts with the pushchair that is closest to her, then Ju-long, and then me. Her mother doesn't bother jumping down from her chair. The kitten walks over to Amanda and then back to the pushchair, which gets a lot of sniffing. When she reaches Julia's feet, she rises up on her hind legs and places her front paws on the feet rest. Julia has been following the kitten with her eyes and now she makes sounds as if she talks to it. The kitten makes sounds too.

Amanda smiles. "Two young girls talking to each other and we don't understand a word of it!"

Ju-long tries to be funny. "Some special girl-code, I suppose!"

Amanda is making tea and fetches some biscuits in a metal cake box. "You are Asians. Were you born here in the UK?"

"We were both born and raised on Hong Kong Island where we went to the same school. My mother is Chinese and my father British. We came to Britain when I was eighteen and my sister, Anna, twelve. Ju-long and I had had no contact since then, until we met again in Hong Kong about two years ago when I visited my grandparents. Dad is in different businesses and mum is an artist, but has worked as my dad's secretary and correspondent for many years. That's how they met."

Ju-long continues. "I study and work at the university in Brighton and work with libraries, where I specially work with Chinese texts and restoration. Luzi works at the university in London and as a freelance writer and editor of books and articles. And you're doing research too. That was how we met again!"

The kitten has become louder, but it looks as if she is afraid to crawl into the pushchair. Ju-long looks at me and I nod. I am sure; he feels Julia's approval too. He kneels, strokes the kitten over the back, slowly lifts her up and places her on Julia's legs. Julia gives a loud cry of joy. Amanda looks scared. She might have thought Julia was afraid.

Ju-long talks in a soft voice. "It's all right, Mrs Fleet. Julia is just excited."

The woman relaxes and pours the tea. I, on the other hand, am more worried about the kitten if baby Julia grabs the fur, because she can have a firm grip. The kitten lies on her tummy purring and crawls slowly towards Julia's face, while Julia reaches out for the kitten. Ju-long sits next to them, so he must take action if needed. I can see he is ready to grab the kitten even though he does not show it.

Julia's hands and Boomers paws are the first to meet. None of them tries to grab the other and the next thing that happens is that Boomer licks Julia's nose. This time she doesn't shout out but uses a gentle laughter. She feels the fur on her face and hands, but she doesn't grab it. They make the connection and Ju-long and I are all tears!

Ju-long comes back to the table while drying his face, but not trying to hide his tears.

Amanda feels a little unsure about the situation.

"Your daughter is young to be so aware of her surroundings."

Ju-long answers her. "Yes. She even looks around when we drive in the car."

"Well, that's impressive!"

I elaborate. "She works hard to grow up. As I told you, she began to walk independently two days ago; on her six-month birthday."

Ju-long has a question. "Mrs Fleet, I guess you have just sold the kitten. What do you suggest us to buy, especially regarding the long fur?"

Amanda gives us her suggestions that are very much in line with what we have read on the Internet, and she repeats that the kitten is not sterilised or spayed, as she says.

230

I sense for a comment from Julia or Sekhmet, but only get a short note. "Boomer will not be sterilised because she will control her pregnancy herself. If she doesn't get into heat, she won't attract any males for that purpose."

I see Amanda gets a thought. "She is used to going outside, so if you want to continue this, you might get a cat door installed."

Ju-long replies to that. "She'll get micro-chipped, which will also control the cat door to not let other cats in."

"Good. The chip is passive and only sends out a signal when scanned. I'll get you her papers and make one on the agreed payment too. Just a moment."

When Amanda leaves, we turn our full attention on the two girls in the pushchair. Boomer seems calm and baby Julia is sensing her new friend to the fullest. Amanda returns with the papers and Ju-long pays her over his phone. He shows her our check and shopping list.

"Mrs Fleet, do you have any comments about this list Luzi and I made this morning?"

She takes the list and looks thoroughly at it for a while. "It looks fine. Here are things you don't need, but they are still nice and will make your and the kitten's life easier. The raw fish is good. Maybe a little raw bird meat from time to time." She smiles. "The water fountain is a good idea too. I wonder if the girl will use it too."

I answer with a smile. "She might. I expect they will teach each other a lot of things."

Amanda just remembers something. "Oh, you'll need a box for the kitten. Just a moment."

She quickly returns with a suitable cardboard box in which she makes some holes with a closed pair of scissors.

When Ju-long reaches down to take the calm kitten, he stops. I sense Julia speaks through him.

"The kitten feels completely safe with her new friend and will be better staying with her during the car drive that I think she hasn't tried before."

I think we might need the box later. "We'll take the box anyway. Her name is Boomer!"

I kneel next to the pushchair and stroke Boomer until I sense she is fully aware. "We'll take you to your new home, where you'll live with us."

She yawns but stays on top of Julia without even standing up. Ju-long slowly drives the pushchair and then we lift it over the doorstep and down to the yard.

Amanda hands me the box and points. "You can go that way and turn left when you get to the street. You can see the parking space and your car from there. Good luck with the new member in the family. I would be glad if you could keep me posted. At least in the beginning."

I wave goodbye to the woman in the doorway. "We will, Amanda."

We soon reach the car without having lost Boomer on the way. After some initial planning, we get them both in the baby chair, even though I must hold Boomer for a short time while Ju-long fixes Julia's belt. Then I place Boomer on Julia and she lies down again. Julia is calm the whole time. I sit in the back with them while Ju-long drives to the pet shop. I call different vets to find one willing to inject a microchip in Boomer right away. The 1066 Veterinary Centre says we can come in an hour, so I agree to that. It might be the time Ju-long will need to do the shopping, and the driving time. I will stay with the girls. I expect Julia to be hungry anytime now. We stop at Pets at Home. Ju-long turns around and looks at me with an uncertain smile.

I smile back. "I'll be all right. I'm sure you'll get a little help."

While Ju-long is shopping, I loosen Julia's belt and get her over on my lap. Boomer follows her new friend and now I pet her gently. She is calm, almost as if drugged. Within a minute, Julia wants her milk, and she suckles and seems to enjoy the present moment as much as Boomer. After a short while, I slip into the same calmness of just being.

I come to the surface when Ju-long opens the back and puts boxes and bags into the car, assisted by two from the shop. Soon after he is in the driver's seat again.

"I can't believe how much space this stuff takes up

for such a small animal. I got a large bed, because I got a clear picture of our two girls sleeping in it and neither of them will keep their present size! Where to now?"

I give the address to him and he types it into the GPS. Then I call the vet to say we are on our way. Somehow, I had expected the vets would be stressed and running around, but everything is calm when we enter. Ju-long is carrying Julia, with Boomer sitting on Julia's tummy, sniffing and looking around.

The young receptionist gets up from her chair behind the desk. "Oh, so sweet. So, this is Boomer I presume?"

Ju-long walks up to her. "Yes, she has been clinging to Julia since they met."

A nurse comes out from the back. "Hello, everyone. I assume it's the one on the top who is here for the chip?"

"Yep, it's Boomer. Luzi, you have her papers?"

"Here they are. We might need a chip on the other one later!"

"The range is only about three hundred feet, so it wouldn't do much good. I've thought of getting my kids GPS trackers. Just kidding! Follow me this way."

It goes fast and Boomer shows no discomfort when the chip is injected. Then a quick registration in the system and we are ready to go home.

Back in the car I wonder. "Ju-long, these last couple of hours seem completely unreal. No conflicts, no drama, just joy and calmness. Would you mind making one last stop at the New Hong Kong Kitchen? Let's do dinner the super easy way today!"

"That'll be fine with me. I might even get a small piece of fresh fish for the new lady of the house!"

"Oh, yes, do that!"

Back home, I carry Boomer on one shoulder and put the food in the oven at a low temperature to keep it warm, and Ju-long changes Julia's nappy.

Now I focus on Boomer's things to get her settled in. I have planned to let the junction point between all bedrooms and bathrooms be Boomer's place.

Boomer's bed seems too large to fit in the junction so it goes in Julia's room with a large blanket. From now on I'll call it "The Boom Box". Her litter box and bowls are in the junction. Here there a closet for the rest of her things too. I wonder if the junction will be a smelly place, but we'll see. There is a ventilation outlet that removes air from the bathrooms and outlets in the other rooms, so that might be sufficient. I put dry food and water in her bowls and sit her down in front of them. She sniffs and drinks a little water. Now she looks around and switches to "adventure mode". I follow her from a short distance, explaining to her in human words what she encounters.

Sekhmet makes connections to the physical world in different ways, but she wants a clear physical connection to this area and does this through Boomer. "And by other means," she adds.

I ask her. "How am I to see Boomer?"

"She is a cat, for now a kitten, and part of my consciousness works through her. Most of the time I'll stimulate her in different ways. And the answer you're really looking for is that I'll make sure she doesn't get badly injured. There will come a time when you'll sense us as Sekhmet/Boomer, and that will be the adult cat, but not just a cat. Right now, you'll enjoy the kitten, Boomer, supervised by me."

Boomer is drawn to the large bathroom and the shower section. I place the shower head on the floor and open a bit for the cold water which becomes extremely interesting.

Ju-long comes with Julia and I shut the water off and place the shower head on the wall.

"I'm hungry. Let's get something to eat. Do you think you can take Boomer with you?"

"Lower Julia and let's see what will happen. Maybe we can put them in the boom box, which I call Boomer's bed. I put it in Julia's room because it was quite large in the junction."

I place Boomer on Julia's legs as she is being held by Ju-long, and he carries them into the boom box.

Julia finds the new place as interesting as Boomer, and Ju-long and I back up, standing in the doorway watching them. I hear Sekhmet/Julia.

"Get something to eat. We'll keep an eye on the girls."

I kneel and kiss them both.

"Mum and Dad, go into the kitchen!"

Ju-long whispers.

"Do you dare leave those two alone? Does Boomer even know where to pee?"

"Why don't we show some confidence in our girls. She might leak a little, but she knows how to use the litter and she is a smart girl. Don't you know, you have only smart girls in the family!"

"I know. Let's get something to eat and then we will sneak in to see what they are doing later."

"Ju-long, I couldn't have done this without you, and it took longer than I expected. If you had spent your day in London, coming home late, the vet would have been closed."

"Luzi, dear, think of the restoration manager who had to be sick for allowing me to get the day off."

Julia is prompt with a comment.

"The library manager had a rough night getting through some of his 'stuff' and gets the day off. If he had allowed things to flow, it would have been easier for him. He gets a cleansing and the break in his routines, which he has been caught in. He is enjoying the day off, if you need to know. He is doing some things he had put aside in his life but loves doing, and greatly benefits from this. At one time, he even had the bizarre thought, 'Maybe I should get sick more often!'"

Ju-long kind of gets the point. "He could just take a day off, now and then."

Julia replies with irony. "You know, Dad? The only reason you should stay home from work is if you are dead sick or highly contagious. If you need a day off, that doesn't count! This is deeply ingrained through generations and in mass consciousness. Your main purpose is to work and make newcomers to the workforce."

"And the joy in life?"

"Oh, we added a pleasure centre during the Atlantis era to take care of that. This centre is so strong that if it is stimulated, you lose your focus on food and procreation. That is why these stimuli must come from food and sex, or else humans will die out."

"So, the stimuli would not necessarily have come from food, drink and sex in the beginning?"

"Oh, we also have clever men in the family, even though they are less in numbers, as mentioned earlier. You're right. If the pleasure centre is stimulated directly, you would be totally passive."

I have a question. "But do some monks not live in total bliss?"

"It is not the pleasure centre, but the joy of the soul."

"Yes, of course. So, in the beginning it might have been the head bands, right?"

"And a clever girl!"

"The clever man has filled his tummy. Can we check on the girls?"

We have only left them alone for about twenty minutes. There is still a little water in the bowl, but most of it is on the floor and some in the dry food. The bowls must be further apart until we get a small fountain. Maybe a plank with two large round holes to keep the bowls where they should be. We also still need a scratching post and the cat door. The latter is not relevant for the next few weeks, as Boomer must build a strong picture of where her home is.

A good thing about not having carpets is that the floors are kept much cleaner. A part of our computer-managed home is the vacuum-cleaner robot and the floor-washer robot. We call them V & W, like the German car brand, Volkswagen.

We find the two adorable girls tucked tightly together, sleeping in the boom box. We pet them gently until they are fully awakened, and then I take up Julia for her milk. I look at Ju-long. "Do you think it will be completely crazy to bathe them both in the bathtub?"

"Yes, I do, but I think we should do it anyway. It will definitely show us if Boomer enjoys bathing. We have the hair brush for her fur afterwards. I'll take that part."

I sense for a reaction from Julia and Sekhmet, but there is no sense of do or don't.

"I'll sit with Julia on the sofa. You can put Boomer in her litter to see if she will use it. I couldn't feel or see anything in the boom box. Let's see if she cares for getting to Julia again."

Ju-long places Boomer in the litter box and she sniffs around a little. I sit down on the sofa, which Boomer can see, even though I have my back to her. Julia has her focus on the milk. Ju-long stands a little aside, trying not to be a distraction to the kitten.

Ju-long reports. "Now she steps out of the litter box without having used it. She sniffs the food and water. Takes no food and only a few licks of water. Oh, remember we have a little piece of fish for her! I guess we serve wet food in the kitchen, right? She looks around. Oh, there are a lot of places to explore! Could you make a tiny whistle? She turned her ears. Try again. Now she turned her head. She has the direction."

I can hear she tries to run on the smooth floor. She will soon learn to retract her claws when moving on the smooth floor and use them where she can

240

get a grip. She comes around the sofa and finds us, miaows, and I sense a combination of a request and a demand. I whistle again. She makes a jump but doesn't make it. I am afraid she will use her claws on the sofa.

"Ju-long, will you lift her up, please. I know she will manage if she gets a few tries, but I mind the sofa."

Sekhmet comments on that. "You must get used to it. Both girls have to be here without you 'minding' THINGS, even small boys."

"You are right. I'll work on that."

"You'd better work fast. Soon you must go to work and Julia will be at Artemis. What then?"

I sense a smile, meaning I don't have to worry. I don't have to go to London all December, and if we both have to leave for a whole day, we must use a babysitter.

Boomer walks over to where Julia and I sit and places herself facing us, in the small groove made by my legs, which I hold together.

Ju-long takes a seat beside us and pets her. "Luzi, I think we should wait with the fish."

I nod.

When I am sure Julia doesn't want more milk she gets time to burp, and then we go to the small bathroom where we keep all Julia's stuff.

I am a little unsure about the water temperature.

"I wonder if the water will be too warm for Boomer. What do you think?"

"We'll keep her in the shallow end. I'll put in the anti-skid mat at Julia's end."

I undress Julia on the changing table and check there is only pee in the nappy, while Ju-long places Boomer in the large bathtub and uses the sprayer head to fill in water after adjusting the temperature. She is very interested in the running water and doesn't mind getting her paws wet. Normally we use a plastic baby bath tub, but it is too small if we have to keep the two girls separate. Julia can hear the water and moves her arms and legs, eager to enjoy the bath. I wipe her below and lift her up.

"We are ready down here. There will be more water in the tub as you continue to use the sprayer."

Boomer has water almost up to her belly, and when I gently place Julia on the mat still holding a hand under her head, her tummy is above water.

Ju-long hands me the sprayer and picks his phone to record this event.

"Let me hold her head. It seems that Boomer is fine."

Indeed, she is. She hits the water sideways with her left front paw and makes small splashes. The same thing must have happened at her water bowl earlier.

I am happy to see that.

"Boomer is confident about the situation!"

Sekhmet brings an interesting comment. "I was there in the water when Julia was born. I relayed that event to Boomer."

Alea the unicorn shows up too.

"I was there as well. Luckily you had got such a large tub! Did you know that you had 9,000+ ascended masters in that tub with you?"

"I sensed a crowd, but I obviously didn't have my focus there!"

Boomer approaches Julia and gives her right big toe a lick, which makes Julia laugh out loud. Boomer moves up along Julia's right side, which is closest to me, and when I spray Julia on her tummy, Boomer licks it.

The water becomes deeper, and now Boomer is almost floating. At one time she gets up on Julia's tummy by first getting on her legs. Up here, Boomer lies down with her head close to Julia's, and they seem to make a deep connection far out of our grasp.

We have them in the bathtub for about fifteen minutes, and the experience has been way over my wildest expectations. I make Julia ready for bed, and Ju-long dries Boomer with a towel and feeds her the small piece of raw fish on a plate in the kitchen.

When I return after tucking in Julia, I hear Ju-long talking in the living room. He sits on the sofa grooming Boomer to clear out her hair after the bath. She likes it immensely and purrs. I take a seat next to Ju-long and lay an arm around his neck.

"This was really a wonderful idea. Even I didn't expect to have another baby in the house so soon. Did she eat all the fish?"

"Yes, she was quite hungry I guess; hadn't eaten since in the morning, maybe."

"Great! I'll call Mum and Dad to tell them the news."

For these occasions, we normally use live feed from the phone's front camera. I call Mum because she is the one most likely to be at home and able to take such a call. She is home, sitting at her computer, reading about 3D printing, and expects Dad home in an hour. Mum becomes enchanted by Boomer and thrilled about the story of how we got her and asks me to send a small clip of Boomer and Ju-long's grooming scene, which I will do when we end the conversation. We are also talking about Grandma and Kong's visit in two weeks. Originally, we had agreed upon spending the Christmas party at Mum and Dad's, but now that we have moved in so early, we would very much like to use it as a housewarming. Grandma will sleep in Julia's room, Kong in the study. Anna will probably choose the sofa, which is also a sleeping sofa, over a hotel room. Mum and Dad will use a hotel or maybe the bed & breakfast they used last time they were here.

Mum agrees. "It is settled then. The women in the family, who attend this meeting, have spoken."

Ju-long smiles. He adores his mother-in-law, as she does him. A scene from the first time she and Dad visited us in London comes to mind. He promises to send a recording of the bathing scene to her as soon as he has made a little editing. We say good-night to Mum and ask her to say hello to Dad.

Boomer has fallen asleep but wakes as Ju-long lifts her up.

"I'll put her in her litter to remind her where it is. If she hasn't found her bed when we are ready to go to bed, I suggest we put her there. I just need to edit the video as promised."

She doesn't seem to use her litter. Then she finds her way into the kitchen—to look for more fish, I suppose—and then she finds her bed. I somehow had expected her to miaow at Julia's cradle, but Se-khmet most likely has directed Boomer to bed.

We have agreed on two signals for Boomer. A one-tone whistle means "come" and a click with the tongue which means "stop". If the tongue click doesn't do it because she is very much into her thing, we will use a clap with the hands. She might be a lion goddess, but she is also a kitten. While Ju-long edits the movie clip, I put the grooming clip in Boomer's folder and send it to Dad and Anna.

The night passes with no incidents, and Julia wakes up at 6 a.m. as she mostly does. I give Boomer, who lies in her boom box, a pet, and she gets up and follows me when I take Julia to breastfeed her in the living room. Ju-long gets up as well, as he has a new arrangement with the manager in London. Ju-long has reported him joyful and well. There is nothing like a rough night and an unexpected day off to change one's perspective or priorities.

I place a pillow as a step for Boomer to use to get to the sofa, which she soon finds out. This time she lies down next to me so I can pet her. I realise that she actually has a strong purr. While sitting here, I get the idea to get a large piece of fish and cut it in thin slices to put in the freezer. It will be easy to take a slice out and it will thaw up in minutes and serve as a fresh meal for Boomer. We can do the same with bird breast and rabbit. To me it is important that the meat comes from wild animals, or ones who have had a good life.

Ju-long will take Julia on his bike to Artemis today on his way to London by train. There has been no snow or freezing-point temperatures, and Julia has assured me that baby Julia is doing fine during the ride. Ju-long likes the short ride as well as I. You wake up in the morning and, in the afternoon, you clear your head getting home from work.

What comes next?

Building of the dome houses has been a major goal for all of us. What we wanted after settling in has mostly been airy thoughts, even for those who had their goals. All this has to take form in the next few months, so we can roll out all the activities in the coming spring.

Ju-long and I have arranged for Sarah and Cloe to come over so we can introduce them to Boomer. When they leave, they seem confident about handling the kitten and they express, that the best thing to do is to be calm and trust in Sekhmet as they trust in Julia.

In the beginning of December, we have our first real meeting about the future of the Dome Home Village. We keep it a closed meeting, but later meetings will be open for the mutual benefit of the community and East Sussex. We expect interest from other parts of the country and the world.

What surprises me is that all have a vision that, beside their personal goals, will benefit the whole. The height of the bar is really lifted by the presence of the non-physical entities and consciousnesses, including the unicorn.

Some talk about the governing of the area; others are more specific and talk about the school system from nursery and up. Some talk about holistic health in all its aspects, and others about farming and gardening of both food and other products.

We are all professionals or skilled, and handy amateurs each in our field.

I have never seen myself as a politician or lobbyist, but I sense I will influence the local government through my involvement in the local community. The human approach of Julia is still waiting in the wings to play her part. I know that in the long run she will leave not only her home but also this area and ultimately the country.

At Julia's seven-month birthday on Friday 6 December, we have a video meeting with Grandma Jiang, seventy-five years old, and Ju-long's dad, Kong, on Hong Kong Island, and Mum and Dad in Sevenoaks. Jiang and Kong will arrive in London on 19 December to attend my thirtieth birthday the next day. Mum and Dad will pick them up. They will spend a night with my parents and drive with them to my birthday the next day. There is a lot of talk about Julia and Boomer.

Boomer has been here for five days now and is moving around very confidently in her new home. She does not quite understand the robots, V & W, but she is not afraid of them or attacking them. She uses her litter box and there have been no accidents regarding this subject, or any other for that matter. She enjoys her raw meat treat in the evening and I guess we have to raise the amount of meat soon and let the dry food be a supplement she can use during the day. Julia doesn't touch the dry food. We have got the fountain that supplies Boomer with fresh running water and also fascinates Julia. They play there together, which is a joy to watch. Boomer sleeps in her boom box at night, and, on the weekends, Julia and she may share it for a short nap during the day. We change the blanket daily. Julia has learned to play "catch the mouse" with Boomer, dragging a toy mouse on strong elastic around the house. For now, we can keep the loose cat hair to a minimum.

Grandma and Kong

I have not been telling much about our family on Hong Kong Island. Grandpa Cheng died last year, eighty years old. Grandma Jiang, seventy-five years old, is the only relative left in Hong Kong that we know of. Ju-long's father, Kong, lived in a mental care home for many years and is divorced from Ju-long's mother, Ting, who is married again. Now Kong is out in the world again and looks forward to meeting his first grandchild. Kong, Ting and her new husband, Cheng, have a good relationship. Grandma and Kong have some activities going with mentally ill people and the elderly.

Dad's parents, Hannah and William, who lived here in the UK, died before I came to England at eighteen years old to start at the university in London.

My family has always attended the western holidays, like Christmas and Easter. Not for religious reasons, even though Mum and her parents are Christians and Dad has been baptised. In Hong Kong we attended both the western New Year and the Chinese Lunar New Year. Our birthdays follow the Gregorian calendar.

As I have told way back, when Dad and his parents came into Mum's family, they respected him for his kindness, equality and respect for all life. He became kind of the new master in the family without acting as one. New habits and traditions came in, one of them being that all family members, after their ability, attend the preparation and cooking of the food and all share it afterwards. His ways became the new standards.

This morning Ju-long serves me an EARLY breakfast in bed. I see the alarm clock showing 5.45 a.m. when he sneaks out of the bedroom. Shortly after, he returns with a salver with my favourite breakfast, a rose in a small crystal vase and a present wrapped in golden paper with a card below it. We can hear Julia, so shortly after he returns with the two girls. I had a few bites before Julia demanded her milk, and then it was time to open the present. Boomer and Julia are playing on top of Ju-long's legs, but Boomer gets very interested in what I am doing when she hears the paper crackle. Ju-long hands them the paper but keeps the ribbon, and they play on.

It is a beautiful rope bib necklace made of soft turquoise-coloured rope about a quarter inch thick, in two sections, and below a large oval pendant with an abstract painting in turquoise nuances covered by a glass diamond. The pendant is encircled in small beads in pink and gold.

"It is from the girls and me. Julia has been a great help in selecting the right one for you. The colours go with your eyes."

I smile and remember her assisting me shopping for materials to paint baby Julia's room.

I read the card from the givers: "To the most extraordinary and wonderful woman and the best mum EVER!"

"Thank you, loved ones. It's so beautiful."

Ju-long reaches over and I give him a big hug and a kiss. I can't move much because of the salver with the flower, coffee and juice.

I see there is a beautiful card in the box as well: "LiePe Jewellery—when jewellery becomes wearable art!"

The artist is Liene Pētersone from Latvia.

Ju-long helps me finish the breakfast and then it is Julia's turn. Ju-long removes the salver and gives me Julia. Boomer lies next to me on her back while I gently pet her tummy. I am still impressed about her strong purr.

Ju-long has been in the shower and takes Julia to make her ready. While I am in the shower, I can hear he talks to Julia about the people who will arrive soon. Julia has demanded a pale-yellow dress. I know it is part of her connection to Kong. Ju-long and I will keep it casual until the afternoon tea.

We have prepared most beforehand, and soon Ju-long will have the dough ready for rolls. I want to save the batter for the pancakes for Dad to make. We have got a lot of large Christmas oranges, and I start up the juicer so the juice will be cold when we serve it. I don't want too much ice in it. I add lemons and a little fresh ginger to freshen and spice it up. When Ju-long made my juice this morning, he used oranges, passionfruit, half a banana and a sprinkle of cane sugar.

Boomer has got an orange collar with blue "diamonds" and a golden name plate. She must get used to wearing it when she moves outdoors. To be honest, I haven't found the right time to let Boomer outside even though we have got the automatic cat door. It is not snowing, but it is still cold and soaked, and the garden is a mud pit. Literally. Most was dug up to place the pipes for the ground heating, and the tank for collecting rainwater is dug down as well. From that perspective, it was not the right time to get a kitten. There are some steel plates painted with white stripes that lead to the front and the back door, and one in front of the garage and an extra to the left of it; not very inviting for a kitten.

Because Grandma and Kong have been flying in the same direction as the sun "moves" they only have a small jetlag. They show up with Mum, Dad and Anna at 10.10 a.m. Ju-long and I have arranged a brunch and we are all washed and trimmed for the occasion.

As the copper-coloured Tesla S stops on the large steel plate close to the front door, Ju-long opens the door to invite the visitors in. Luckily it is not raining, and the wind has calm down. I stay behind him with Julia and Boomer on each arm. Mum and Grandma are the first to arrive. Mum is carrying a plastic bag and her coat. She steps aside to let Grandma come in first. She gets a hug from Ju-long. I can sense he fears to squeeze the fragile woman too tightly. I have to put down the girls to give Grandma a proper welcome. "She is getting older," I think. I take her coat and she finds her indoor shoes in her bag. Then she kneels to level up with Julia who makes a sound and looks her straight in the eyes.

"Oh, my adorable grandchild. You're truly your own!"

She pulls her close and holds her for a while. Julia is totally calm. As soon as Grandma lets go, Julia makes a sound again. Boomer squeezes in to be part of the hugging ceremony.

"Oh, hello, Boomer. You're a pretty little thing, but there are stories about you, so I know your small size is only in your physical appearance."

I take Mum's coat and put it on a hanger, while she puts on her indoor shoes. Then we hug.

"Happy birthday, Luzi. It is the first time you receive me in your finished new home."

I can hear Anna and Kong outside. Kong comes in and gives his son a hug. "Congratulations with your new family and home. I am happy to see it works out so well."

"Thanks, Dad. Come in and let me take your coat."

He has his indoor shoes in an inner pocket in his jacket. Very practical. Now he moves forward to me and I just catch Dad's eyes as he comes in and closes the front door.

"Welcome, dear Kong. It is so good to see you again in person!"

"Oh, and here is my granddaughter, Julia!"

He actually sits on the floor and lets Julia come to him. Boomer is soon to follow.

"I assume you chose the dress yourself, am I right? It's very much like the first time I saw you."

"Sure she did. If you can get a female, orange, long-haired Maine Coon kitten, a yellow dress is no big deal!"

It pleases me to see people's levels down to Julia instead of lifting her up and passing her around. Now Anna and Dad come to me, wishing me a happy birthday, and give their hugs. Then Ju-long joins in and all are sitting on the floor. Amazing. There is some initial talking, but then I address Dad.

"Dad, brunch is almost ready, but we still need the batter for the pancakes."

"Leave that to the professionals, young woman!"

Ju-long follows him into the kitchen area. The kitchen is open to the dining area, which is part of the living room, so we still have contact.

"Kong, will you pick up Julia and I'll give you all a tour around the dome?"

I see Grandma is very attached to Boomer, and she picks up the fur ball. Boomer turns her belly up when lying like a baby in Grandma's arm. That is new to me.

Sekhmet elaborates on the situation. "When she holds Julia, it reminds her of the time when she was a young mother, but carrying Boomer reminds her when she was a baby herself being held by her mother. It even goes further back; back to the animal kingdom; back to the beginning. In that sense, she's close to the beginning; the beginning lying just past her transition from this life."

They are all truly impressed about this very different house. I promise Kong that his son will explain the more technical aspects of it. Dad will, with no doubt, join in.

Ju-long announces, "Brunch is ready. Take a seat. Grandparents can't sit next to Julia, because they'll spoil her!"

I know it is a joke, which tells me that he is thrilled and very much himself, or he would have said nothing like that.

Anna is fast to reply. "Because the father to the just-mentioned individual wants all the spoil for himself!"

He laughs. "You're not easy to fool, sis. You may be the biggest spoiler of them all!"

Julia sits at her highchair at the head of the table and I quickly arrange the guests.

"Grandma at one side and Kong at the other side

of Julia. Ju-long faces Kong, and Anna, Grandma. Mum next to Ju-long and Dad next to Anna. I'll take the other head of the table. This way I can conduct everything and watch everyone's moves."

Anna salutes me with a frown, looking very serious. "Aye, aye, Captain."

Julia has eight teeth now and her swallowing reflexes work excellently for mashed food. She can't use a spoon, but with guiding she can handle a feeding cup if the food is blended and able to flow out of the spout. We feed her with a spoon. She is good with finger foods as well. I sometimes, for a second, feel her impatience with her muscular precision.

After brunch, Anna and Grandma prepare Julia for a nap. Boomer is not into a nap. She can get too much attention from the people who have moved to the living room after cleaning up.

Grandma and Anna return. Kong, Ju-long and Dad walk to the laundry room where all the technical stuff is installed. After the inspection, they get Kong's and Grandma's stuff from the car and put it in their rooms. I am curious to see how Grandma will do, sharing the room with Julia and Boomer. I think she will love it. They arrive with presents for me as well.

I have placed the necklace I got from Ju-long and the girls on the table. We all gather in the living room and I open my presents.

From Anna I get earrings with three turquoise

stones in different sizes hanging down on a small pin, the smallest lowest. This suits the three-level necklace from Ju-long, Julia and Boomer. Did she get some guidance? I sense a smile from Julia.

Grandma and Kong give me practical outdoor clothes for both gardening and walking in nature. Very appropriate.

Mum and Dad give me a gift voucher for trekking boots or whatever I feel I need most. It wouldn't make any sense to buy me boots that probably wouldn't fit anyway.

They all get hugs and I put on the necklace and the earrings and it looks great.

Ju-long and I have made no Christmas decorations. We will do so with the rest of the family. There will be no Christmas tree. We have got red and white ribbons, some evergreen twigs like mistletoe, holly, laurel, fir and yew, and other things from nature, including spruce cones and reindeer moss. There are clay and wire and a lot of other stuff to use, including templates of straw to make wreathes and a large, two-feet-in-diameter template of steel wire for a kissing bough to hang down from the top of the dome. There is already a large hook in place and a socket to plug in a wire with a light bulb. The kissing bough will hang on a chain.

As we start out with the project, I talk a little about Alea the unicorn, Artemis, Pan and Sekhmet. I tell that Artemis, Pan and Alea set the base sense or feeling for the event. "They pointed out that they are always present, as are the crystal, or Christ consciousness, represented by Alea."

Anna lights up. "So, it's always Christmas?"

"Yes, dear, it's always Christmas!"

"With food, presents and everything?"

Sekhmet brings through a comment. "If you choose, dear. If you choose. Why shouldn't every day not be a celebration?"

Even though Anna is twenty-four now, she has always brought forth the joy of her child in her life. In that sense I hope that she will never grow up.

At some point I see that Boomer has fallen asleep on her back next to Grandma. Her white furry tummy moves up and down as she breathes.

Julia wakes up, and I breastfeed her in her room. After burping her I change her nappy and put on her dress. Now she is ready to go out, charming the world. She walks into the living room while I clean up the bathroom. I can hear the adults when they see her. The princess has arrived on the scene.

Dad wants to make waffles with ice-cream, or whatever one prefers for the afternoon tea, so he and Mum take over the kitchen.

When we sit with the tea and waffles, we talk about how Julia named Boomer.

Anna has a question. "Wouldn't baby Julia give all of us names in her own sense of a name to identify us?"

Julia connects with Anna who relays the conversation. "Baby Julia for the most part names people from how they express joy. Dad, or her granddad, is WUUW, the sound you cry out when you slide down a snow-covered hill on your butt."

I slip in a comment on that. "It's a future event she has shared with me."

Anna continues, "Mum, her grandma, is a tough one, because this is the sound of blue and white sparkles, like when you open a box of magic. It could be 'sparkle' for short."

Now Anna laughs out loud. "Aunty Anna is 'UMM'. The only thing you can say when you have taken the first mouthful of your favourite food."

I know that Anna at the same time gets a love-wash from Julia and is greatly moved to tears.

I can't help myself. "The truth comes from little children!"

Anna dries her eyes and continues, "Grandma, her great grandma, is the sound of a small stream with golden flashes of the sun in the water. It could be 'gurgle' or 'chuckle'."

It reminds me of Julia's own sound. "The sound she makes when she is in joy."

"And Kong. It is the sense you get when you look into the night sky and realise that the stars are right there for you to touch. Some kind of awe like WOW, when you realise that distance is an illusion.

"Ju-long is clearly the sound of the sea. Both when you are above the water and under the surface. The most prevalent sound is a deep rumble, but there is much more to it. Hmm, the beat of the heart of a huge whale. Big-heart!

"Julia about herself. In a way it's a perfect silence. The silence of ALL.

"Luzi, her mother. The ever-stream of light. The sound of streaming light. It is very much like the feeling she has about herself. You may call it Eternal Love."

We are all very moved after this. It is obvious that baby Julia's awareness works on many levels or with multiple senses and that she is in touch with her I Am and Master Wisdom.

At the end of the afternoon we have even finished the huge kissing bough. Ju-long will put it up later, when he gets the ladder from the room in the back of the garage. Mum, Dad and Anna leave, but will be back on Christmas day, 25 December, and stay overnight. Dad has arranged Mum and his stay-over.

Kong helps Ju-long with the ladder to put up the kissing bough. I hoist it up with a rope around the hook and then Ju-long attaches the chain to the hook, removes the rope and plugs in the light. It all works fine. This is our Christmas tree. We have two wreathes. One goes on the outside of the front door and the other one goes at the entrance door in the living room, so we can see it from there. There are some decorations on the walls, replacing pictures for the moment. There are some on the tall tables where little girls shouldn't go. Some of them contain battery-powered lights.

Kong is very interested in the dome technique so Ju-long and Jacob have arranged for him to visit inside Jacob's geodesic house tomorrow. It is basically built out of large wood triangles and covered with wooden roof shingles. Each shingle is made of compressed wood, which makes them more weatherproof. The whole construction is very organic.

The next morning Grandma gets up at the same time as Julia. She is used to getting up early and can report that to her knowledge no foul things had been going on during the night. Not long after, Kong shows up as well. Today it is the fourth Sunday in Advent, 22 December, and we have an early breakfast. It is still dark outside and Julia is fascinated by the large dome of the kissing bough that shines light out from the inside. It looks a little like a green planet which shines the light of its core out through the crust. Boomer plays with one of her toys under the table so she is part of the gathering.

Ju-long and I have agreed to feed Boomer fish or meat morning and evening and leave her the dry food to be accessible the rest of the time. The luxury dry food contains meat too. We have a small date list on the refrigerator to set check marks so we don't both feed her. Sekhmet is her health monitor, so everything is well under control.

After breakfast we have the bathing show with Julia and Boomer in the bathtub. This time we have extra hands, especially for grooming Boomer afterwards. The two girls are very relaxed after this and we enjoy each other's company. At some point Julong and Kong go visiting Jacob to see their house. When they return, Kong carries a tree trunk with a few short branches.

"This will become a scratching tree for Boomer. I just need a solid base because she can grow quite large, I hear."

I look at the tree trunk for a bit. "You could clear the branches on one side and attached the tree to the wall somewhere in the junction."

"Not a bad idea. But will it be here she will need it, or is it where she spends most of her time or where she wakes up? Maybe I can split it in two so we put one in the junction and one beside her bed."

"That sounds like a good idea, Kong."

Ju-long throws in a grandiose plan. "What if we get a really huge tree in the living room and use it as decoration at the same time?"

I turn on my practical side. "I guess it must wait until spring. Right now, everything is wet and dirty."

Kong comes up with an idea. "But you can look for a suitable tree for the purpose."

Ju-long and Kong work on splitting the tree. I guess it is more work than they had expected, but they are persistent, and Boomer ends up having two scratching trees wound with rope. It is lovely to see father and son working so good together.

I move my story to Christmas Day, 25 December, when Mum, Dad and Anna will arrive for Christmas dinner, which will be at about 1 p.m. They arrive early to be part of making dinner. It will be a partly British Christmas dinner with roasted turkey, but with Christmas cake rather than pudding. There will be no Christmas crackers, but special fortune cookies.

Julia wears a red dress and looks adorable when she walks around on her short legs. Boomer might move more elegantly, but she still lacks the majestic moves of a grown-up cat. Julia is barefoot, which makes it easier for her to keep her balance and feel the floor. The floor is of wood and heated, and her feet aren't cold. She and Boomer greet the guests as they arrive. Anna first, heavily loaded with her large bag and some plastic bags, probably Mum and Dad's. She hands them over to Ju-long, who comes to assist her.

"These are for the kitchen."

She moves a little away from the door and sits down on the floor. Julia and Boomer invade her. "Here are my lovely girls!"

Now Mum and Dad come in. They are heavily

loaded as well and Dad heads right for the kitchen. Mum puts down her bags and walks around to all of us.

"Hello, everyone, and a merry Christmas to all of you."

Dad picks up Mum's bags and carries them to the kitchen. I know that Dad's homemade Christmas cake is there somewhere. Then he makes a round as well. They both end up on the floor with Anna, Julia and Boomer.

Because we all had an early breakfast, Ju-long and I place different foods on the kitchen counter towards the dining area and living room. Here is tea, coffee, juice and water.

We meet in the kitchen to pick tasks. Luckily things don't have the same preparing and cooking time, so we don't have to be seven adults in the kitchen at the same time.

Anna sets the table, assisted by Julia. She finds out that she can carry Julia in her baby sling facing outwards, so Julia always can have her focus on what Anna is doing. Anna tells her everything she does. To Julia it is as if she is doing it herself. What a great idea. Thanks for the tip, sis. Later, I see they are making place cards, drawing everyone's face and writing their name.

The Christmas dinner is ready well before scheduled and people have changed to their chosen outfits.

Grandma wears a rose blouse, a shawl in a darker rose colour, and a purple skirt mixed in with some white.

Kong wears a green suit, a white shirt and a bluish tie.

Mum has chosen a traditional Chinese dress in red and gold.

Dad wears a dark-blue shirt with a light-blue pattern line and rolled up sleeves, no tie and dark pants.

Anna wears a rose-ruffle V-neck dress with a floral print.

Ju-long has chosen a white shirt and a waistcoat with a dark-blue butterfly pattern, and dark-blue pants.

I end up choosing a champagne-coloured sleeveless dress with colourful flowers and a narrow golden belt.

We share Christmas gifts in the afternoon. I will only mention those from Grandma and Kong to the rest of us, because they are so unique.

From Grandma, Ju-long and I get two large Chinese fan embroideries of her own making for hanging on a wall in the living room. Julia gets a smaller one for her room. Grandma has also thrown in a few training chopsticks when the time comes for her to train using those. I hope they will meet again before that.

Grandma gives Anna a medium-sized fan with her own embroidery in the same style as the ones for Julia, Ju-long and me.

From Grandma, Mum gets a beautiful natural jade bracelet, handmade by an elder where she lives now.

I understand Grandma's challenge that she expresses when she hands her present to Dad. "And, Carl, what to give a man who has everything he needs and wants?" What emerges from the wrapping is a handwritten and hand-painted book in Chinese and English. A real gem of art.

Grandma gives Kong an exclusive set of oil paints in the colours he uses most. "An artist shouldn't run out of materials! I didn't dare to buy any brushes because you fancy special ones and even make ones yourself."

From Kong, Ju-long and I get a portrait-oriented framed painting on a goat's skin. It shows a traditional scene from a Chinese harbour in old times with ships and sales booths, nets hanging to dry and many other details. The colours are mostly in blue nuances with some white. The frame is about half an inch thick and in dark-blue lacquer.

From Kong, Mum and Dad get a snuff bottle, beautifully decorated from the inside with a garden motif.

Kong's gift to Anna is a wood carving of a young woman, where he has added some paint to emphasise the carving. The title would be "the free spirit" and is a perfect match for my sister.

Kong's handmade gift to Julia is a traditional Chinese painting of a little girl and her kitten playing outside. There is also a Lei Feng hat with imitation fur—the smallest I have ever seen—for the cold season.

Kong gives Grandma a traditional brush painting on rice paper of an old couple sitting under an apple tree full of apples. There are some animals and birds around. To me it looks like a reunion, but I don't say it out loud.

When I look at those handmade gifts, I am amazed that Grandma and Kong have had the time to produce these art pieces. Even just one would have amazed me. Dad had arranged to ship all the gifts from Hong Kong.

Kong and Grandma help Julia hang up the fan and the picture in her room. Both level with her eyes so she can look at them or take them down if she pleases. A little later she gets her milk and a nap in her cradle. Boomer is already in her boom box.

Sometime during the afternoon, I stop for a moment to look around at the people in the room. This is a Chinese home and Dad is the only 100 percent Caucasian. I have never looked at myself as an easterner or a westerner, white or yellow. These are just attributes to separate people, not to unite them, except in those groups.

We have Christmas tea at 5 p.m. Cakes and cookies, biscuits and rolls with butter, cheese or jam and mince pies with meat or vegetables. There are different kinds of coffee, tea and hot chocolate, with whipped cream. We play some games as well as playing with Julia and Boomer, and we take a lot of photos along with video clips. We find time to sing some songs as well.

At the end of the day, Julia is tired and falls asleep almost instantly when Anna tucks her in. When Boomer has got her raw turkey meat, Grandma tucks her in. She has been quite active during the day and has had a lot of attention.

We spend the evening telling stories, playing a few games and looking at the different Christmas gifts. I am most impressed by the handwritten and hand-painted book Dad got from Grandma. Each page or double page is filled mostly with an image followed by a short explanation in Chinese, also translated to English, placed discreetly so it doesn't disturb the art. The interesting thing is that you can see each page or double page as a story in itself, and you can read the book as a continuous story. Grandma doesn't seem to be willing to tell us where she got the book, and the author's name is clearly not authentic.

When it is time to go to bed, Anna prepares the sofa in the living room, Grandma sleeps with the girls, and Kong uses the study. Dad has got a room at

Northrise Lodge Bed & Breakfast. They only need to sleep there one night and don't require breakfast. It is the same place they used last time they stayed over. They leave through the laundry, using the back door, and walk the two hundred yards to the B&B.

Next morning Julia wakes up late. The time is almost 7 a.m. Mum and Dad arrive shortly after and start to prepare the breakfast. I think the dough for the rolls was made last evening, but I am not sure. I serve fish for Boomer and set a check mark on the list so no one else feeds her. Julia has already got her milk and is ready to take in the day.

Today our guests will leave. Grandma and Kong will fly back to Hong Kong tomorrow and Mum and Dad will drive them to the airport.

Before lunch we take a walk to the Clive Vale Angling Club reservoirs via Barley Lane and a shortcut. I hope Boomer will behave, being home alone. We will be gone for about an hour.

The ground is dry, and the temperature is low, but no frost. There is only a light wind and the sun can shine through the clouds about half of the time. Julia, sitting in the pushchair, wears the Lei Feng hat she got from Kong. I gave her a simple cotton bonnet with a snap lock beneath to make sure the hat is pleasant to wear. As we walk down Barley Lane, we see they have been working on moving trees and earthwork to prepare for broadening the road. Jacob has told us that the trees next to Shear

Barn Camping will be moved a few yards into their lot. If some trees can't be moved because of their roots, new large trees will be planted instead. The machinery has been moved aside, waiting for the personnel to return in the new year. We meet other people taking a walk; many with a dog on a leash.

It is a fresh and reviving walk, but it is nice to return to our warm home. We have worked up an appetite and there are a lot of leftovers we can use for lunch. Boomer seems to have slept all the time. At least there are no traces of her being active. She approaches us as we come in and Ju-long gives Julia the mouse-on-an-elastic so she can play a little with the kitten. Seeing people walking with their dog, I wonder if we should train Boomer to wear a harness for a leash. Will it even make sense to walk with a cat like this? Dogs may go crazy when they see her. When she grows up, she might be able to fight off even the largest dog, but that is not the point.

Our guests drive off after lunch. It has been a wonderful Christmas, especially to see Kong and Grandma. As always, I wonder if it is the last time I will see Grandma, but not in a sad way. I know that Anna feels the same; probably Mum and Dad too. Anna will spend New Year's Eve with our parents. For our part, we have plans to snuggle up at the wood burner on New Year's Eve, all four of us.

Great and grand things are awaiting us in 2020, as 2019 has been a year with much change and clearing for new things to set foot and root. I sense the area will be more united and people will feel they are part of a giant entity. Is it in reality Britannia who shows her presence, joined with the other loving friends? The land is being cleared and so are people's minds. This way they become more aware of a deeper connection to all we call life. The unicorn has truly returned.

The End

I hope you have enjoyed the book and ask you to take a moment to make a short review on your favourite retailer website.

Thanks in advance, Eriqa Queen.

On the next page, you'll find my short comments about this book.

Author's Comments

If you haven't read the previous books, you may find that some subjects are not covered sufficiently, but this is the way I chose to present this material.

I give special thanks to the sovereign consciousness that, in this book, is named Saint Germain, for his huge contribution to mediate the wisdom to both myself and the reader.

It has been a challenge for me only to present one subject at a time, since much of what I want to tell you depends on each other to give you clarity of what I speak.

Writing from the light

Here I will tell you how I create the material that will end up being a book.

To start a project

I usually start out with an idea, a working title. This idea has an etherical but dormant counterpart. As I start to put words, usually the title, to my manuscript, the idea becomes active. This creates a sparkle of consciousness in the imaginative realm. This is how all creations starts.

I may use time trying out different fonts that might suit the title. In this way, I softly blow the ember, being the sparkle of consciousness, and other ideas are being attracted to the sparkle from the vast soup of possibilities.

This is an intuitive, nonmental way of writing. My mind does not create the story and is often surprised, even perplexed, about what is being put into the manuscript.

The sparkle becomes a light while more ideas are drawn into it. Characters emerge with their own personalities and the first contact is very special. Again, it is not a mind thing, but a heart thing. I connect and feel the character. Sometimes I know (like in knowingness, which again isn't a mind thing) that the character is there, but it takes some time or the right conditions in the plot before the character opens and joins the plot. It is quite fascinating.

My way of writing

Imagine a dead tree trunk without branches lying on the forest floor. It has two ends, but let one of them be a start. When I write something, anywhere in the story, it's like planting a flower seat somewhere on this tree trunk. I don't know exactly where I plant it, and I might move it to a different location later on.

Chapters or headlines and sub-headlines are made along the way and I can move or change everything.

I use colour markings for different purposes.

If I am somewhere in the story that doesn't seem to flow, I need to wait for the flow to this place or I could make another connection for a part ready to flow when I tap into it. You can imagine possibility bubbles coming floating towards the light. If they haven't docked, they are not accessible.

A lot of research is done, including Google Earth, street view, 360-degree photos, videos, reviews and articles. I KNOW what the places look like, and views of non-accessible places are delivered from the "light" with all human senses and more. I know the characters in the same way and with much more than their looks.

I must deliver parts of a story, and I can clearly feel when I and my mind have to do the job ourselves; it's a huge difference! There is usually no help to get … this is MY part, my responsibility.

The story is ready for proofreading when the light gives me the sense of it being ready.

Additional stuff

Yahtzee with seven dice

7 dice Yahtzee	How to score	Score
Aces	Count and add only aces	
Twos	Count and add only twos	
Threes	Count and add only threes	
Fours	Count and add only fours	
Fives	Count and add only fives	
Sixes	Count and add only sixes	
Sum (84 if 4 of each)		
Bonus (50)	Only if 4 of each dice type	
Total upper section		
1 pair	Total of the pair	
2 pairs	Total of the 2 pairs	
3 pairs	Total of the 3 pairs	
3 of a kind	Total of the 3	
4 of a kind	Total of the 4	
5 of a kind	Total of the 5	
6 of a kind	Total of the 6	
House (2 + 3)	2 of a kind + 3 of a kind	
3 + 3	2 times 3 of a kind	
Full house (3 + 4)	3 of a kind + 4 of a kind	
Straight (1 ... 6)	25	
Chance	Total of all dice	
Yahtzee (75)	All 7 dice are sixes	
Total lower section		
Grand total		

The following music, film, books and links are a continuous list from the previous books in the series.

Links

Chinese Unicorn: chinese-unicorn.com

Dome houses: https://www.the-self-build-guide. co.uk/dome-houses/

Music

The soul, the Master and the human are in different ways represented in these songs.

Alan Walker, "Faded", 2015. Vocals performed by Iselin Solheim.

Beatles, "Here Comes the Sun", 1969, performed by Sheryl Crow, 2007.

Corrs, "Would You be Happier", 2002.

Cut'n'move, "I'm alive", 2000.

Eurythmics, "When Tomorrow Comes", 1986.

Joan Osborne, "One of Us", 1995.

Nena, "In Meinem Leben", Nena Kerner, 2009.

Nena, "Tokyo", 2010.

O-Zone, "Dragostea Din Tei", 2003 (not the English, but the Romanian version). See a translation on the Internet.

Shaina Noll, "How could anyone", written by Libby Roderick.

Shakira, "Try Everything" (From *Zootopia*), written by Tor Erik Hermansen, Mikkel Storleer Eriksen and Sia Kate Isobelle Furler.

Suzanne Vega, "Gypsy", 1987.

Books

Running from Safety – An Adventure of the Spirit, Richard Bach, William Morrow and Company, Inc., 1994

Films

Battlestar Galactica, TV series, 2004.

Cirque du Soleil: Worlds Away, 2012.

The documentary part of *Time of the Sixth Sun – dreaming ourselves awake*, 2019.

www.ingramcontent.com/pod-product-compliance
Lightning Source LLC
Chambersburg PA
CBHW020100310726
48970CB00002B/416